The Reluctant Assassin

Also by Johnny Payne

Confessions of a Gentleman Killer
The Hard Side of the River
Vassal
Heaven of Ashes

Johnny Payne's

The Reluctant Assassin

BY

Étienne D'Abattoir

Dispatches Editions

Toronto / 2021

Some of these essays first appeared in *Dispatches from the Poetry Wars*

LCCN : 2021932458
ISBN 978-1-952419-92-8

Dispatches Editions is an imprint of Spuyten Duyvil Press
Write to: poetrywardispatch@gmail.com

The Muse

IT WAS MID-SUMMER IN DUBROVNIK. Giselle and I sat on the terrace of a restaurant overlooking the Adriatic. The early full moon was disappearing behind a cloud like—well, all the good similes have been taken, so I'll say, "like a coin being dropped into a slot." The problem with similes is that they're always like something else.

Giselle and I had met in the underground. She was playing the ukulele—I don't know where she'd even gotten it. I had enough money to get through the spring and summer—I had an embarrassingly small trust fund, the portion leftover to the family member who refuses to fight it out with the rest. I invited her along. Mostly we made love and ate, cooking for each other the two or three dishes each of us knew, approximating the ingredients with whatever we could rustle from the couple of food shops in the walled city.

I was writing the manuscript *Suivre*, which was promptly acquired, received four glowing reviews, got translated into sixteen languages, and was read poorly in all of them, after which it went out of print in French in less than two years. In other words, success. The truth is, Giselle wrote a substantial portion of *Suivre* without ever reading a word of it. She would half-lie on the bed, languidly alert (if that's possible), a copy of a Mina Loy book downturned on her lap, and periodically call out bursts of words, which I would incorporate into the text. When the manuscript was complete, I insisted that she and I would be co-authors. She trenchantly refused. "That would make me a surrealist or a Dadaist, and I can't stand either. I would have pushed Duchamp's head into his urinal if I'd ever got the chance."

I didn't contradict her. But secretly, I resolved to remove all traces of her words, otherwise be counted a plagiarist. I printed out the entire text and began crossing out words with a pen. I soon realized I didn't remember which words were hers and which mine. It was possible I was erasing myself entirely from the manuscript, leaving only her presence. Was it possible that we had begun to think alike, to speak alike? Was our romantic connection turning us into a single individual, erasing all separation, the goal of the Romantics?

"Stop stressing," she said, sitting up. She had guessed my secret. "You're not a plagiarist. I don't want the book to be mine. I'd much rather serve as your muse. Isn't that why you brought me?" It was. I had never thought of it consciously, but I nodded my head dumbly. "So we're both getting what we need."

I kept writing through the next two months, our routines unaltered. Giselle never spoke of the future or of any obligations. She seemed unhurried, as if this were the only reality. Then the manuscript was done—really done. I knew it and she felt it from my body language and the way I picked at my nails.

"Let's have one more trip to our favorite overlook."

We went to the terrace and watched the moon drop behind a cloud; the wind picked up and I offered her my jacket. She smiled and let me drape it over her. "You look exactly like Dora Maar."

Giselle seemed pleased. "Do I?" She had dressed up for the evening, in a slinky black dress I didn't know she owned, one entirely too skimpy for the weather. She shivered deliciously and pulled my coat closer around her after rolling back the sleeves to uncover her hands. Before lighting her Gauloise, she took out a gold cigarette holder, a slender tube several inches long like a tiny trumpet, with a black Bakelite mouthpiece and a flaring bell, into which she studiedly inserted the end of her cigarette. She'd said she'd gotten it from a pawn shop and claimed it had once belonged to Picasso's tortured muse. She had remarkably beautiful hands, the fingers exceptionally slender and graceful.

"You would have fitted perfectly into café society in her time."

Giselle blew a contemptuous smoke ring. "Café society is kindergarten for artists. And surrealism is art therapy." Then, staring out at the blue-black twilight, the sailboats in the harbor disappearing from our sight, she began to recite.

> Today it's another landscape in this
> Sunday at the end
> of the month of March 1942 in Paris
> the silence is
> so great that the songs of the tame
> birds are like little
> flames you can see. I am desperate
> But let it be.

"Are you desperate, untamed little bird?"

"No. But Dora was."

"I'll keep working on the book. I can add more poems. And I still have some money left."

"As you wish. You know this is only going to last until we go back to Paris. I will have served my purpose."

"But I love you."

"Don't cheapen our interlude with that sentimental cliché. I left my boyfriend to come with you. Though he's probably onto someone else by now."

I wanted to come up with a sharp retort. But in what remained of the light, I could see an incurable sadness in her eyes, one I hadn't put there, nor could I take it away. Instead, I answered with the words of Joyce Mansour.

Happy are the solitary ones
Those who sow the sky in the avid sand
Those who seek the living under the skirts of the wind
Those who run panting after an evaporated dream
For they are the salt of the earth
Happy are the lookouts over the ocean of the desert
Those who pursue the fennec beyond the mirage
The winged sun loses its feathers on the horizon
The eternal summer laughs at the wet grave
And if a loud cry resounds in the bedridden rocks
No one hears it no one.

"You said it best, Étienne. I'm going to assume that's one of the poems you wrote about me."

I didn't contradict her. "Would you like to read the manuscript? You might have suggestions."

Her face was now in shadow, only her feet still touching a ray of light. "I don't have to read it. I am it."

In Translation

For a time, I became obsessed with trouvières, those 12th century songsters. Whether we French writers will or not, they're our predecessors, lutes at the ready, throats in voice. Long before the Symbolists took hold with their dense allusiveness and cryptic imagery, verse was closer to the ground. Writers and troubadours said plainly what was on their minds and hearts. I gravitated to them as a parched man kneels before a rivulet. A particular short lyric by Guiot de Provins created the straightforward poetry I needed after my breakup with Giselle.

Las! toz jors la desir,
Et ades voi ma mort,
Et si ne puis morir.

Alas! forever I desire her
And always see my death
And cannot die.

I ditched Paris and began working in Brussels as a commercial translator, making bankers and diplomats sound as if they had souls. I returned to a passage in George Steiner. *Our own being is modified by each occurrence of comprehensive appropriation. No language imports without risk of being transformed.* That was my challenge—to let words act on me, rather than trying to control them.

You'd think that after ten-hour stretches of business and government translation into and out of French and Italian, I'd want nothing more than a beer and a detective movie. I might have gone out on the boulevard, had I known anyone. But I did not, and the least of my inclinations was to sit at an outdoor table alone, glancing at the fabric of each passing skirt and the legs that carried it past me. So I found myself hunched over my desk in the dubious light, on the border of eyestrain, trying to make sense of Folquet de Marselha.

The more I tried to decipher Provençal, the less I understood.

> *Be an mort e lor*
> *Mei huel galiador,*
> *Per ques tanh qu'ab else plor,*
> *Pks ylh so an merit,*
> *Que'en tal don'an chausit*
> *Don't han fach fallimen,*
> *E qui n'aut pueia bas deissen!*

It was unlikely I would find a Provençal dictionary in a bookstore at that late hour, or any hour. To look online would break the magic spell of my desolation. I wasn't willing to give up loneliness until I knew what would take its place. And for that, only a thumbed-through tome bearing a human touch could suit my soul.

Two displacements allowed me to write. I decided to translate his poem into English, the language of reason—of things making sense—and to use phonetic translation, roughly matching sound for sound, rather than sense for sense.

> I would have been dead, my Lord
> But the gladiator fled
> Because I cried so hard.
> Well, I have no merits
> Except chasing women.
> Don't have faith; I'm fallen.
> Yet how beautiful my demerits.

It was all wrong. I'm not good at dying, only pretending to. And *gladiator*, that's too harsh, mere melodrama, certainly not a suitable metaphor for Giselle. Crying, I only do it softly. And I don't chase women. Fallen, yes, as Adam was, I suppose. But really, more than anything, crestfallen. The one true line was the last one. Not sin, not lack, not failure. Simply demerits, as a child gets in grammar school, for putting the verb in the wrong tense. And beautiful ones! I began to laugh at my preposterous translation, which seemed a comedy that Guillaume Apollinaire might have enjoyed, had he smoked some hashish beforehand. I ended up gently mocking myself, a decent poet but the worst of translators. Why couldn't I complete Steiner's hermeneutic motion? Because I didn't want to expose myself to the risk of memory. Yet that was the only way out, sincere remembrance, no tricks.

I went back to Steiner. *The dialectic of embodiment entails the possibility that we may be consumed.* That is exactly what I wanted to express—what had happened to me, how I was annulled, such that I ended up in Brussels poring over speeches and contracts like a miserable scrivener. It was her I wished to recapture, if only for a moment, and I had to do it as trouvières do. I sat and wrote without thinking, without even trying. The words passed through my body, making me whole again.

Her love runs through my heart, its flume
As clear as any mountain stream
Shaking the leaves of the wild rose
While from a branch, a nightingale
Brims with song, its beak a spout
Pouring its trill into the waters.

Its notes can't be grasped; they flow too fast.
Meadows sigh in their mist, the field a pond
The tree a mast. Her scent refreshes
The forest, its speed heals my wounds
And though she's gone, a liquid wisp
Clings to me, a drop left on my skin.

I paced around the room, rereading, and though I had no lute to accompany my voice, I opened the window and sang to the street below, ebullient, over and over until somebody called up from the sidewalk for me to shut up and get over it.

EL MISTERIO NADAL

cannot but read this splendid rescued (reconstructed?) book--perhaps a roman á clef—putatively introduced by Bolaño, without thinking of Ricardo Piglia's recension of a quote from André Gide speaking of his novel *Les Faux Monnayeurs*, within Piglia's apocryphal novel *La historia de un asesino inmune*:

> *Le style des Faux-Monnayeurs ne doit présenter aucun intérêt de surface, aucune saillie. Tout doit être dit de la manière la plus plate, celle qui fera dire à certains jongleurs: que trouvez-vous à admirer là-dedans?*

When I struggled with this issue with my novel *L'Horloge Redondante*, I first adopted a version of Nabokov and Beckett's solution, translating the manuscript into various languages, to no good effect, as I tried to recreate the tedium at the heart of my novel, only to find it becoming more and more interesting the more I passed from French to Spanish to English to (competent) Russian to (passable) German to (abominable) Farsi. It was then I had to accept my fate as an excellent stylist, with all the attendant prejudices and snobbery implied therein. Or, in words taken from those benighted pages,

> *Chaque fois que le carillon sonnait, je fus piégé dans sa résonance, stupéfait á quel point le passage de douze á douze, de minuit á minuit était facile.*

Bolaño became relevant to my life circa 2005, when I taught seminars to wickedly talented Latin American young writers, self-displaced in Avignon, not so much in exile as waiting out the year to see what happened next. Yet we were at odds over Bolaño, whose work had burst onto the scene posthumously, making him their writer of choice. My favorite student, a male sylph with an unwarranted confidence, bought me a copy of *Los Detectives Salvajes*. I found its descriptions of bar life, fucking, and wandering, desultory and third order, and the dialogue pretentiously uninspired. I then tried *2666*. Worse. It almost made me stop writing, so much did I abhor it. The constant name-dropping of philosophers was a substitute for actual thought. The anti-intellectualism felt lazy and warmed over. My range of literary and analytic reference was annulled by this situation. I argued with my students that this lowering of the bar was characteristic of them, to whom I had tried with mixed success to teach the work of Levi-Strauss, Paz, and Heidegger. They seemed not to value anything from more than half a generation before their own time, or further away than the end of the hall where the drinking fountain sat. The Boom had left them with a bad taste in their mouths; they needed to slay the father; they didn't want to write epics. They wanted to write small, domestic, mindless stories, in an apolitical manner. There were no odysseys, only rambles.

As I returned to my writing desk one night, discouraged, staring at the blank screen, I recalled the words of the under-appreciated A. J. Ayer:

> By following our accepted standards of proof, we sometimes arrive at beliefs which turn out to be false.

I tried again. I stopped looking for adornments, architecture, polyvalence, and incisive insights. The most I could keep down was *Estrella Distante*, in part because of its modesty of length. My students graduated and I also moved on. Then I began to watch, with alarm, a proliferation of posthumous works by Bolaño, as the adulation of his work surpassed the ecstasy formerly reserved for the brilliant, elegant, modest Borges. Was Bolaño in the pantheon? Would his reputation outlast that of Cortázar? Would his relatively shapeless books, diaries, essays be compared favorably with those of the ruthlessly organized Vargas Llosa? Or was this only an affair of the heart, with premature death crystallizing its splendor?

Then, into my hands came the volume that is the subject of this discourse, and at its center, Vladimir Nadal. **El Misterio Nadal: Purportedly Compiled and with Introduction in 2001 by Roberto Bolaño.**

It arrived, unbidden, anonymously sent, and out of its pages slipped a letter dated November 1, 2018. It was addressed to Nicolas Moguilevsky and recounted the letter-writer's experience "hanging out" (as the Americans say), in Barrio Palermo, where I once also spent several pleasant afternoons. It was simply signed "Kent." I assumed that it was from the infamous book-giving, petard-hurling, hoax-perpetrating imp Kent Johnson, whose reputation for pranks (and let it be said, literary generosity) exceeds that of Leopoldo Lugones, who once got a rarely tipsy Borges to wade in a fountain in Garibaldi Square at midnight, having convinced him that it was the Fountain of Youth.

No matter. This book gave me unexpected hope that the younger generation was not entirely wrong in its objects of adoration, to the extent I began a series of literary travesties of Li Shang Yin's poetry, in a newly profane spirit.

> *You ask how long before I come. Talk about pressure.*
> *The night rains on Mount Pa swell the autumn pool.*
> *I think you know what that means. Trim a candle at the West window,*
> *As the lash of water on the pane makes me thirsty for a beer.*

El Misterio Nadal gives me (false?) hope as Nadal gets situated against an entertaining rogue's gallery, not the least Benjamin Péret. Again, Gide's novel:

> *Je sens en moi, confusément, des aspirations extraordinaires, des sortes de lames de fond, des mouvements, des agitations incompréhensibles, et que je ne veux pas chercher à comprendre, que je ne veux même pas observer, par crainte de les empêcher de se produire.*

Bolaño kicks off the book with becoming nonchalance, remembering the impressive drinking prowess of this mere acquaintance. *He drank three grappas, fairly fast; in that respect, he fit my faint memory, though if I'd seen him on the street, I wouldn't have recognized him.* Literary palaver follows in a bar. *Where the fuck did you hear about my next book?* And they reminisce about imagined harmless pranks such as kidnapping Octavio Paz. I wish they had, if only to test whether Paz had the *huevos* to have them both assassinated later, thus proving his *hombría mexicana.* The Infras would truly have passed into history. For as we know, Latin America is the pinnacle of martyrdom. However, only Benjamin Péret, my countryman, was decisive enough to throw a drink on Paz. *Vive la France!* To his eternal credit, Nadal did break the arm of a strategically placed street punk, while Bolaño gave the other a roundhouse.

Bolaño's introduction to Péret sets the stage for letters, poems and essays that seem to put every significant "counter" writer of Latin America on crossing paths, some of which lead to Soviet Russia, Europe and America. One feels the force, the epoch, the energy, the excess, the tempests in scalding teapots, the name-dropping, the bomb-dropping, the pants-dropping of Surrealists, Infrarealists, and other partisans who collectively, with their loquacity and dense yet casual range of nomenclature reference, make the "real" Nadal recede before us as a mere textual effect, a product of informed gossip. A typical head-spinning sentence:

> Stalin's only daughter, Svetlana Alliluyeva, ended up in Spring Green,
> Wisconsin, in the late 1960s, unofficially adopted by (Frank Lloyd)
> Wright's wife after Mamah, the mad, Theosophical zealot Olgivanna,
> and there Svetlana still is.

This book represents six degrees of separation, in that everyone, no matter how "minor," is connected to numerous world-shakers. In fact, in this volume, there is no such thing as being minor. If you were there, you mattered. However militantly one movement or cadre opposes the other, there is no meritocracy, no ultimate ranking. Many times, literature seems a pretext for living—as it should be!—for ending up in the bed or in the bar, and in that sense, this compendium is an apologia for a lost time, no less suffused with longing and nostalgia for *le temps perdu* than is Proust's great work. One of my favorite letter writers herein, Laura Puig, describes making love with Nadal in her mother's bed, watching television until the mother discovers them, Nadal coolly talking his way out of the situation, and the mother clearly attracted to him. Such a discomfiture, turned to advantage, in this tome counts as paradise.

Faced with such a Babel of sentiments, both trenchant and soft in *la république des lettres*, I can only cite Proust, who, perhaps as a result of my erstwhile abortive self-translation, now comes to my mind in English, not even my second-best language.

> A fashionable milieu is one in which everybody's opinion is made up of the opinion of all the others. Has everybody a different opinion? Then it is a literary milieu.

To my eminent surprise, this pellucid volume awakened in me a range of literary emotion I have not experienced in quite some time. In the unforgettable words of Man Ray, "Don't put my name on it. These are merely documents I make."

Drinking Celan's Black Milk

T HERE IS A TIME TO BE WRY AND A TIME TO BE PLAIN. And though I am not religious, there's a time to be silent and a time to speak, as Ecclesiastes tells us. I have been thinking about holocausts. Normally, with reverence, we recognize only one—The Holocaust. In a sense, that wicked devastation deserves its perverse pride of place. By another token, it is right to remember the Armenian Holocaust, the Cambodian Killing Fields, the Rwandan Genocide and the one in Darfur. To say nothing of the slaughter of indigenous people in what is now the U.S., and the unwitting extermination by disease of up to 90% of those in South America during the Spanish colonization. And then there's Stalin. The list could be longer still. Let's stop before we get to the ancient world, before the mind is overwhelmed into paralysis and a deadening of compassion. In a sense, it is more respectful to recognize all the Holocausts. Why? Because to say there is only one means that phenomenon was historical, it passed, and now we're okay. The memorials built are exactly to remind us that mass cruelty happens in many places, regularly, and the idea of remembering is so that such atrocities won't happen again.

I don't like to think of such things. I'm an aesthete by nature; I don't wish my politics in the fore. I consider them a private matter, like my sexuality. My sense of propriety is a comfortable jacket—sometimes a straitjacket. Yet, as is the case with many others, politics in America is being forced upon me by circumstances. And the consciousness that a holocaust can happen anywhere at any time, is not hysteria nor paranoia. Many recognize the signs and signals of what could become one. The degradation of the human by a racial category; denigration to the point of mass violence and seething hatred both personal and in the aggregate, is the first step to madness and yes—genocide. It doesn't have to be ten million, or six, or one, or even half a million. Perhaps it could be ten thousand. There's no such thing as a petite holocaust. Let's not quibble about numbers. Let's simply say white supremacy is the new state fair, and at the 4-H booth, slaughter is in the air.

Why am I thinking about these matters now, other than the fact that they're as patent as the tarry smell of fresh asphalt when you walk on it and feel your soles just slightly hesitate in the sponge, and you imagine that beneath it there could lie a sinkhole leading to the center of the earth. But no, I mean why right now instead of five minutes ago? Because of "Deathfugue." I hadn't read Paul Célan for a while. I'd instead been reading Lord Byron, as one watches an action movie with CGI cars that explode yet do no actual harm. I opened the pages, almost by happenstance, when I came across an edition on my bookshelf, long neglected, and the opening words struck me—forgive me Célan, but I believe your poem can be—dare I say "culturally appropriated," in the best sense, by many of us, albeit we or our relatives were not burned to ashes?

> Black milk of morning we drink you at dusktime
> we drink you at noontime and dawntime we drink you at night
> we drink and drink
> we scoop out a grave in the sky where it's roomy to lie
> There's a man in this house who cultivates snakes and who writes
> who writes when it's nightfall *nach Deutschland*

Having read those verses, I wanted immediately to unread them. It was as though Célan had slapped me in the face as a do-nothing dandy. I was angry at him, struck mute for a full ten minutes. I wanted to shout back that it wasn't my fault. Then I imagined him answering "Well it's my fault.

Why shouldn't it be yours? And have these matters disappeared from human consciousness or action? If so, I apologize."

My wit and humor fail me today. I am as somber as a clock that refuses to do anything but tell time. I had a housekeeper for a while when I lived on the border in El Paso, Texas. Surely a strange destination for me, not to live in one of the world's capitals, but I was taken there by romantic love and found I could freelance edit and live well in such an inexpensive place. Then I fell in love with its landscape, the tiny blue wildflowers that decorated its austere mountainsides in spring; its mute cactus silently drawing sustenance from the earth; its dry arroyos promising a flood.

My housekeeper—I paid her more than the going rate, but probably still not enough. We became friends, ate breakfast and lunch together each Friday when she came and she would stay until late afternoon, the cleaning done, until I drove her down the border highway and dropped her off so she could cross into Mexico on foot. She cooked for me *gorditas*, *pozole*, and *chile colorado*. Hilda mounted a blistering, sardonically humorous discourse as we sat eating, about the many slights she received from the border guards each day and how she pushed back with scorn. The constant sense of idle threat, of arbitrary mocking, pervaded her many crossings, wearing her down mentally, creating ongoing existential uncertainty. She was strong, yet deep in her heart, a step from being nullified.

She called me one time, distraught, because her grandchild and other school children had been taken hostage by criminals. They wanted $2000 from each of the parents (or in her case, grandparent). This sum was unconscionable, given her income. I offered help with that, and how she got the rest, I don't know. They wanted to meet her late at night, in a cemetery out beyond a maquiladora. Hilda was designated to go on behalf of all the parents, carrying everyone's money, as she had the strongest stomach of the group. Or maybe she just volunteered. I offered to accompany her, because I didn't want her to go alone. She refused, telling me that nothing would be gained, and if those people found out who I was, they might come and kill me and my girlfriend. She promised me she would be safe. All they wanted was the money. These kidnappings were a regular occurrence and if they'd wanted to kill the children, they would already have done so and they could just as easily go to her house and kill her and her husband.

She went and recovered the children, but their fingertips had been burned, as if to erase the being of each.

> He calls play that death thing more sweetly
> Death is a gang-boss *aus Deutschland*
> he calls scrape that fiddle more darkly then hover like smoke in the air
> then scoop out a grave in the clouds where it's roomy to lie

But then there's this:

> Curve a space
> that there may be speech, of earth,
> of ardor, of
> things with eyes, even
> here, where you read me blind.

Today I want to write something that matters, a poem for the ages, a poem that someone else will find by accident, on a page deep within a book, and it will remind him or her that what's going on can be stopped—yes, by actions, but also by words, the right words. It all begins with words, before the beatings, the smashed possessions, the deportations, the crematoriums, the ashes of what could have been a beautiful civilization.

Ballad of the Devil's Fart

I WAS RAISED ON PROPRIETY. My father, a mathematician, treated life the same way he did a theorem or an equation; logical, formal, and tending toward a predictable outcome. I never heard my mother, a seamstress and part-time opera soprano, say a curse word, not even while singing in a foreign language. They were not Puritanical; they simply lived as they believed, while not judging others. Both had been brought up in relative poverty and believed that good manners and straight thinking, as much as talent and hard work, would lead to a satisfactory outcome. Mostly it did. They tolerated my restless habits, my dreamy eschewal of thinking about "a profession." They assumed I'd make my way, which I did.

The one thing my mother wouldn't tolerate was vulgarity. That's not to say my father didn't curse, for curse he did, especially when trying to solve nearly insoluble equations. My mother was understanding of my father's penchant for throwing back in an easy chair, playing too loudly what she called "saucy" ballads, such as "The Trap," sung by the incomparable Brigitte Bardot.

> *Sur la plage abandonnée*
> *Coquillages et crustacés*
> *Qui l'eût crû!*

> On the abandoned beach
> Shellfish and crustaceans
> Who'd believe it?

As I, the child, lay on the carpet reading a comic book, alongside him, as he sang along and tried to suppress his tears, I tried hard to understand what might be saucy about this song, as my mother shook her head. She would give my father a kiss on the crown and leave the room. Once, my father shot me a glance and said, "My iniquity," as if that explained anything.

Later—and it was always this same song—when "La Madrague" was done for the evening, and my father switched it off, leaving us in silence, my mother would drift down the stairs, having changed into a pretty night garment and a matching, translucent robe, smelling of shampoo and a hint of perfume. I thought it strange, the first time this happened, that she would put on perfume at that time of night. My father would stand up, call me in for a hug, and upstairs they'd go, without any thought of putting me to bed. They just closed their bedroom door. I fended for myself on those occasions, eating ice cream out of the carton and falling asleep in his chair.

That was propriety in my household. They never would have approved of my titling an essay "Ballad of the Devil's Fart." If they were still alive, my mother would make a point of not reading it, or if she did, of putting a ruler over the title, so she could rename it in her mind, something operatic, like "Satan's Stench," or "A Ballad of Sulphur." But I cannot take credit for this impish heading. The phrase comes from François Villon. That poem either was never written, or it qualifies as one of his lost compositions.

It was in fact my father who put me onto Villon, though he never mentioned the man's name, or that he was a poet. We were shoveling snow, before it had a chance to freeze and it had become a sweaty business. When we took a break, my father, seeing I was in a foul mood, gave me a sip of sweet coffee from his thermos, and without provocation, recited precisely, in medieval French, what I took to be some sort of limerick that might be spouted in a tavern.

> *Puis paix se faict, et me lasche ung gros pet*
> *Plus enflée qu'ung vlimeux scarbot.*
> *Riant, m'assiet le poing sur mon sommet,*
> *Gogo me dit, et me fiert le jambot.*

Peace is made, she lets off a thick fart,
more swollen than a dung beetle's poison
She whacks me on the head, the laughing tart
And grabs my thigh, begins to joke again.

He achieved his objective, which was to take me out of my sulky humor and make me laugh. I had him repeat the stanza, twice, until I could get the gist, then committed it to memory. I asked him, disingenuously, what the verse was about. "Men and women," he said simply. "Don't recite it to your mother."

This Villon is my preferred of the two poets whom scholars speak of today. When I eventually read "*Mais où sont les neiges d'anten?*" (But where are the snows of yesteryear?), I found that famous line rather boring. Snow lay within it, to be sure. Still, it didn't bear the bittersweet taste of coffee on a snowy morning when your fingers are getting numb through the gloves.

Ambrose Bierce was outraged when a religious-leaning editor republished in book form his newspaper column, named *The Devil's Dictionary*, as *The Cynic's Word Book*—which was promptly aped by many other would-be "cynics"—cynically. In restoring to the book its original title in a 1911 edition, Bierce commented that after so much bad imitation by others, he didn't want to be accused of plagiarism by anyone, on account of the sin of being the original author. The definitions are clever, and acid tipped.

> Blackguard, n. A man whose qualities, prepared for display like a box of berries in a market—the fine ones on top—have been opened on the wrong side. An inverted gentleman.

The idea of an "inverted gentleman" appeals to me a great deal. For who is a gentleman? He who disguises—not his entire nature, but part of it, with manners. From that understanding derives the adjective "mannered," e.g. insincere, a parody of refinement and discretion, which betrays itself by being overly insistent. Yet one's nature is not entirely base, therefore the ring of the sinister does not necessarily obtain, even to obstreperously polite individuals whose insincerity is patent. Those who carry themselves better than others should not automatically be assumed dissemblers. We (yes, I shall put myself in this category) don't wish to inflict our ugly traits on our brethren under the spurious guise of "honesty." That would be the true dissembling, the notion that we are "being authentic" by exercising borderline offensive behavior. I will never be the one to plop into someone's booth at a diner and start in on some low-grade disclosure of childhood discomfiture (or "trauma," as is more popular stateside, in the land of therapy). The English are often tweaked for the lack of this extrovert's trait, their reticence in fact overstated as being buttoned up. Whereas we French get let off the hook as theatrical, eccentric to a person, likely to eat soup out of your bowl in a fit of enthusiasm, creating a combination of farce and drama in our wake, like Carnival confetti strewn over an Our Lady of Lourdes procession. We are just as reticent as the English—and when I say "we," in either case, I always mean "some of us," for louts and prigs exist in all places, and ultimately, the idea of a national character is grossly overstated.

So, refinement—and yet. It may be that a dose of Villon might be the medicine for its superfluity. If I'm honest, I'm no less polemical than the next human over. I just don't want to get into a shouting match about my beliefs. I tend to understand polemic as a philosophical method of elegant rebuttal between two persons who will bring fiery intelligence to a conversation, therefore they don't have to raise their voices. Then they go out together for a drink after, as lovers do. I had such a conversation with a seller of fish tacos in Ensenada, where I'd gone to wade in the surf and possibly take a vigorous swim. This man, Pedro was his first name, hadn't read Rousseau, but he might as well have. He had a perfect understanding of the origin of civil society. His neighbor, while fencing in his own property, had enclosed part of Pedro's plot of land, whether accidentally or not.

He mentioned this possible oversight to the man, who ignored him. He mentioned it again, with the same result. At that point, his impulse was to burn the man's house down. He had even gone to his shed and picked up a six-liter gasoline can. Then he thought better of it, because he believes that people are essentially good. He would wait the matter out. I asked him whether this generous view had yielded results yet. He said "No." I argued for a less than sanguine appraisal of the man's intentions, a Hobbesian view that people are constrained only by laws from committing all kinds of depredations. Pedro shrugged and answered, "I know him. He'll come around." I won't say he and I came to agreement. But our fifteen-minute polemic left us both satisfied. By not challenging him beyond tolerance, knowing when to back off, I became Rousseau for a spell, tacitly endorsing his goodness in not burning down the neighbor's house, and giving him time to change his mind.

Part of me wants to be Villon, provoking duels, forging papers, discharging the Devil's Fart without shame, laughing about it while a free-handed woman grabs my thigh. An inverted gentleman might well speak with what my mother might have called "sulfur breath," or more pointedly, the Devil's—well, you understand what I'm saying. Villon has his own phrase. I envy his robust depiction of humanity, borne partly out of a life of fighting, drinking, whoring, getting jailed and having the king free him. The marriage of form and plain speaking is dizzying.

In frost or hail, my bread gets cooked.
I am debauched, she follows suit.
Which one is best? We're even matched.
Cat and mouse compete in sloth.
We relish filth, so filth surrounds us.
We flee honor, and honor flees us,
In this brothel where we hunker.

I wouldn't know how to begin writing such a poem. The first time I visited a prostitute—given, I was only seventeen—I asked afterward whether she'd had a nice time, and was laughed out of the room, out of the brothel, onto the street where passersby smirked, somehow privy to my stupidity. Of course, I immediately went home and took a shower, not so much trying to clean the event off my skin, as wash away my naiveté.

Ballad of the Devil's Fart

Villon plunges his hands into the warm, throbbing intestines of life. Then he eats them, somehow still appearing as a person of delicacy, because he cleverly rhymes *esclat*, *escript*, and *estat*. I believe that someone who doesn't read French at all will appreciate him better, as the sounds roll past, the harmony so complete that his hymn to a bawd could easily be mistaken for the Sunday sermon of a country pastor.

If I dared to begin such a ballad, how would I start? From Ambrose Bierce, there is this.

> Feast, n. A festival. A religious celebration usually signalized by gluttony and drunkenness, frequently in honor of some holy person distinguished for abstemiousness.

On my first trip to New Orleans, I went to hear jazz and ended up getting madly drunk with a group of strangers, and groping a woman who offered her delights—okay, her cunt—in someone's Latin Quarter apartment where we were packed in, half of those in attendance out on the balcony watching the Saints go marching. I do remember that, appropriately, the Dirty Dozen Brass Band was playing "Walk on Gilded Splinters." I only recall half of what we did, but it was more than enough. First attempt:

> Booze-breathed, I fumble for a hook
> Where back meets nape, a wanton crook
> Whose crime she fast abets, her speed
> Exceeding my coarse carnal need.
>
> No one looking finds it weird.
> They belch approval, toke on weed
> Throat acid trailing my first kiss
> As firecracker follows fuse.
>
> My head throbs tomorrow's regret
> While she searches my front pocket
> Whether for money or for flesh.
> Either way, our parts get meshed.

Onlookers don't find couch tricks gross
Au contraire, the crowd's engrossed
By our slobber, grunts, cries, bliss
While I soon feel I have to piss.

Pulses of tuba exuberance
Blast from street below, flatulence
Made musical, and a gold trumpet
Heralding our Jericho's strumpet.

She grabs my thigh, says "There's the boy,"
As we rush through a brief orgy
Adding our hump to the excess
That both of us were born to bless.

Villon would tell me I'm too elegant for my own good, but I think he'd like
the tuba exuberance, the gold trumpet and my rhyming "piss" with "bliss."
It was a raunchy episode I preferred to forget—then again, why should I?
I'd call it slime with rhyme, but I don't want to judge. The inverted gentleman only tells what was.

❧

Bierce again: *Exile, n. One who serves his country by residing abroad but is not
an ambassador.*

I consider myself a citizen of the world. I have always aspired to be inter-
national, whether at home or in one of the multiple countries in which I've
lived. I like to think of myself as a less dyspeptic Gombrowicz. On the
other hand, those caustic tendencies, coupled with his real and undeniable
passion, are what give him his distinct voice. He is a gadfly, discontent in
his very bones, and without something to chafe against, he would cease to
exist. Yet who is more Polish than him? He spent his somewhat accidental exile in Argentina sending works, whether novels or essays and reviews
tinged with diatribe or polemic, back to Poland, for a Polish audience,
mostly writers, so by one measure he could not be more parochial.

In this, we are different. I now write as much in English as French, and in other languages as well at times, such as Spanish. And translate from still others—honestly, sometimes I forget the difference between translation and "original" writing. The gap between the world's best translator and the world's worst plagiarist is slender. My audience is—whoever will read my work. It's not an epistle. I write and fling the result to the wind. Sometimes the wind slaps it back in my face.

Examined carefully, I could not be more French. It could be because I look back so much at compatriot poets from previous centuries, committing the sophistry of believing that those eras "no longer exist" so that I can perpetrate the fiction that they're not really French, therefore I am not a Francophile. But I am. It's a new breed—the French exile who admires France as a distant, virgin star to worship.

What to do with this great freedom? No one has challenged me, because I haven't rubbed their face in it. It's difficult, even if you wanted, because social media has erased epistolary culture. Email eroded it. With Twitter, it's gone. I defy anyone to express an original thought on Twitter. I don't mean to blame social media for annihilating our inner lives—though it largely has. The truth is, even in a non-epistolary culture, I still write, as I once did, introspective letters to a few close friends, while avoiding petitions to be signed. I am not an instantaneous person. Some friends have lauded me for being "lightning quick." I don't believe that to be the case. A thought forms in me slowly, for minutes, hours, days, or weeks, I'm not even aware of it. And when the right moment comes, I let it fly. I am as surprised as anyone at my quip or sudden insight.

To be an ambassador while residing abroad, I'd have to postulate an us and a them, and I am not above observing that Americans, as a breed, are evangelicals. There are two kinds: secular and religious. The two have minimal differences between them; howbeit they might disagree among themselves, together they know what's good for everybody else. Europe is far too tolerant of this tendency, and indulges, despite their apparent criticisms and scathing derision for the United States, in a bizarre hero-worship; a love-hate relationship. It's one of the many reasons I couldn't live in my native country anymore. I'd rather live in Los Angeles and draw my own conclusions.

I've done a few takedowns, but I am not qualified to offer sustained political commentary, of which there is already a plethora. As for demonstrations, I went to one that allegedly aligned with my way of thinking. I grew bored with the chanting after five minutes and tried to strike up thoughtful conversation with some of the attendees. I was not well received. No one was available for a fine sifting of the issue at hand. I took a sign that was handed to me to shut me up and began to shout the exact same thing as everybody else was shouting. Only then did I receive welcoming head shakes. I was one of them. The protest ended, with a few arrests, and as I was not among the arrested, I went home, as did all those who didn't go to jail. There were no farewells or "see you next time." It was as if a movie shoot had ended, or an elevator had reached the first floor.

I am more in the mold of Rabelais, in *Gargantua and Pantagruel*: "It is agreeable with the nature of man to long after things forbidden and to desire what is denied us." That sentiment won't make the evening news or get adopted by either side of a standoff in its platform. There is a big difference between *it's our right* (true, clear justice) and *to long after things forbidden* (murky commitment, vaguely biblical, redolent of taboo and primal scenes, possibly a dark and not forward-thinking outlook). In everyday life, on practical matters, my politics are clear. I am a progressive humanist with occasional radical tendencies. But how I express that is much less straightforward.

Villon the sybarite and reprobate wasn't political in any sense except calling in favors to get himself out of scrapes. Yet he would fit in much better at many protests. He'd spit on the ground, grab a sign, approach the truncheon-bearing police, shout out for them to go fuck themselves, advancing fearlessly, never a backward step, backhanding one or two, until they grabbed him and beat him and cracked his skull. And dragged him off to jail with his more reasonable mates who were trying to get a specific point across. It wouldn't have been his first time in jail, the previous stays due to petty theft and other small criminal activities. Still, he would be the one fêted after a pro-bono attorney bailed him out, lauded for his valor in the field.

In the end, I am nobody's good citizen, nobody's ambassador. Such is the lot of us skeptics. We're on no one's team. I am no Alexis de Tocqueville, with his stammering platitudes, trying to sound statesmanlike, his flights of oratorical rapture ("I sought for the greatness and genius of America in her commodious harbors and her ample rivers – and it was not there") and his one-size-fits-all perorations. Some of his aphorisms sound like lyrics discarded by John Lee Hooker. ("It ignores the body and goes straight for the soul.") If we were traveling together and he said he was my cousin, I would disavow all knowledge of his person. To even aspire to be a man without a country is beyond his imagination. He spends every page of his sage tome giving a scolding blessing to America from his French perch.

How do I serve my country? By not purporting to speak for anyone. Rather, speaking against, with strategy. Respecting the prerogatives of language in itself. Parody, pastiche, burlesque, and travesty, done softly. Those are the weapons, beyond reasoned discourse, of a reluctant assassin. That's what Brecht offered: a travesty of justice. Not a *depiction* of a travesty, which would simply be mimetic—the opposite of what he stood for. The purposeless erosion of language is the enemy, an erosion perpetrated by the many, protected by the few, the esoteric, the standoffish, whose thoughts are dismissed because they are too inward, not enough of a thunderstroke, not sufficiently trenchant for any of the many who presume to speak for the masses. Constant certitude? Heaven protect me.

As compelling to me as "The Ballad of the Devil's Fart" is Saint John of the Cross, in "Falconry," closing in on understanding (what he knows as God):
To pounce on the bird quick and true
In flurries of high interplay,

I soared so dizzy a way
I was barely a guess in the blue.
Even so, at the zenith of hope
I hung numb, until buoyant on love
In thrilling crescendo above
--a prize!—on the plumage I swoop!

The modesty of perceiving oneself as "a guess in the blue" is compelling,
more so than being marked out by others in a fixed state.

I find unexpected counterparts. The best way is to page through magazines,
without looking for anything. Then sometimes, it's there. Most recently, a
poem by the queer, feminist Kenyan poet Alexis Teyie.

Mapenzi Si Shurua, Huja Yakaja

The night you leave, the sky breaks out
in stars. They burn like open sores.
The acacia, scarred from private wars,
still has leaves.
I am not radical in my sorrow.
What has come before,
that which has been handed down—
these are my only methods.
I feel what I feel should be felt.
I say nothing new, nothing different.
My concerns are as they were before:
is the tea too cold to drink?

To feel the stars as sores, yet not be radical in sorrow, is an ideal state. The
combination of passionate engagement, with a self-saving detachment;
that's not being numb, nor evading the issue. There are searing moments in
which the possibility of emotional annihilation supersedes the occasion—
the unnamed yet cherished person leaving, the town being burned, getting
fleeced of your savings. At a given instant, the ever-present external condi-
tions that threaten to crush the soul and body, are less than the power those

closest to us wield, and so a wound translates into "private wars." The only question being, "is the tea too cold to drink?" There is nothing to decry, no one to push back against. One simply is, as one was before. It is Augustine's *idipsum*. Everlasting self-sameness, the sheer act of apprehension. God as a pronoun. Metaphysics as modesty. If ever there were an adequate answer to the call of the Devil's trumpet, it's this.

Teyie's poem is the antidote to existential numbness. "I say nothing new, nothing different. /My concerns are as they were before." In her lines, one senses neither activism nor retreat, and even less, mere stoic endurance. Rather, we get thoughtful quiescence. It may be a prelude, but to what, we don't know yet, and it's not our business to force the moment. Maybe the you's departure brought on the sorrow; maybe it was there already. The refusal to declare either way is a radical gesture of another kind.

Reasons I don't like the Marseillaise:
    1) It is a mindless call to action.
    2) It is cloaked in the dubious romanticism surrounding the French
       Revolution and has long since been co-opted.
    3) Its lyrics are disturbing.
    4) It is almost interchangeable with all other national anthems.
    5) People like to sing it in soccer stadiums.
You don't have to be a diffident expatriate to cringe at these lyrics:
    To arms, citizens!
    Form your battalions
    Let's march, let's march
    That their impure blood
    Should water our fields.
I don't know whose blood is impure, then or now, but martial conflict precipitated by allegations of impure blood doesn't usually end well for the impure ones. Thus, I fart diabolically on the flag of my nation, into which I was born by accident, and to whom I owe nor concede any fealty. The best

thing it gave me, besides my parents, is French as a first language, thus access to the beautiful and bestial poetry of my literary forbears.

⸎

Let us understand the difficulty of writing like Villon. One drole M. Bombardon (o blatant pseudonym!), in 1878, set himself the task of treading where the deliriously profane one trod. The price of the volume he published was 25 centimes. There is no record of a Monsieur Bombardon in the literary annals, (no doubt he would have corrected this mirthfully to "anals") except the information listed on the pamphlet's cover that he was Professor of Schlingrophone at Petardian University. So, a wag. The slender volume's name?

Le Pet, poème lyrique, Satirique, Humoristique, et Rigolard

The Fart: a lyrical, satirical, humoristical and funny poem.

As with jokes, it's ill-advised to advertise in advance that what you're about to tell is funny. You're usually signaling that it's not. But, let's have at it for a couple of stanzas.

> One has sung of the *gaudriole*
> One has sung of Bacchus the God
> One has sung of the *faribole*
> But from Parnassus, I gauge,
> Never before has this peak
> Produced from its sweet foliage
> The aroma of an escaping fart.
>
> Strange shots at our heels
> And we're mighty astonished
> When we're surprised, and feel
> It just striking our noses.
> Pushing aside all in its way.
> Imitating the roar of the cannon
> It bounces along the shore
> As it escapes its prison.

And so it goes on for 24 vainglorious rhymed French octets in perfectly mechanical iambic tetrameter. We are treated to a celebration of different kinds of farts: shingle, musical, timid, brutal, accompanied by a host of percussive metaphors. The poet clearly had a good time writing it, and certain friends doubtless, among cups of wine, were inclined to chortle at their poetical friend's clever take on something they all could relate to. Elegantly, M. Bombardon ends, as do most of the great poems of classical antiquity, with an envoi to the Muse.

> Since everyone here refuses
> The sweet scent of my incense
> Come into my arms, my dear muse,
> Come swoon soul's accents.
> Because it's yours, my adored one,
> For whom I intend these verses,
> Fly to the empyrean,
> I want to follow you there with my farts.

On the one hand, this repetitive, schematic, humorless, self-congratulatory, wink-wink, ready-made-for-the-smoking-room-chair exercise fails as poetry on every possible level. One should read this right before tackling Pope's *The Rape of the Lock*, to understand how brilliant the latter is. Mock-heroic odes are not as easy as they look. To write in this manner even passably, you must first prove competent at writing actual heroic verse (in couplets, to keep the clamps on your wit) that does not simply ape the tired tropes of antiquity, palaces reduced to ruins. You have to be smart to play dumb. A touch of the disingenuous and the deadpan would be necessary, or flashes of sincerity, rather than jocularity and laughing at one's own jokes before the audience can.

On the other hand, the poem could have been—dare I say it?—a gas. It might have become, in more nimble hands, a rhapsody reminding us that we're all children when it comes to le pet, that there is an essential mystery to why this bodily function, of the many, is the most amusing. At its heart is the child's first passage from innocence into the social world, with its rules and taboos of what you can and cannot do in company. A spontaneous fart is the one least likely to get you in trouble; the most likely to raise a smile—unless you do it once too often, in the wrong crowd.

There is nothing winning or provoking wonder or surprise in this self-amused inventory, to elicit more than the bark of a fellow after he exclaims "That's a good one!" There are only two legitimate ways to go—the child's view—or Villon. Villon's style is comparable to that of Franz Hals's painting "The Gypsy Girl." So vibrant and earthy is the portrait that the lyricist Lennaert Nijgh wrote an "artless" and charming song about her.

> You stroll through the streets, follow the thieves' trail
> With beggars and soldiers, with theirs hats over one ear
> You pull your skirt up and laugh at every man
> Who dares to do in the dark, what can't be done in daylight
> And by night your name goes around
> In the pubs here
> By the blond foaming beer.

Silly Babs, its subject, is another Fat Margot, boisterously taking the poet in her arms while he celebrates their mutual drool.

I was on holiday in the Pyrenees, in the town of Llo, soaking in Les Bains de Dorres, the sulfurous hot springs at the Sègre Gorge, right beneath snowy peaks. There is nothing as enfolding as that. Eschewing the new, I'd opted

The Gypsy Girl

for the antique baths made of granite blocks. I had skied and now it was time to stanch the budding ache before it blossomed, by drawing that light pain out into the 40-degree Centigrade water. I find it curious that sulfur should be associated with the Devil. As with many substances, its smell is not inherently unpleasant. It's a question of its level of concentration. The faint, agreeable scent of sulfur was pulling me toward a mindless state, something I cultivate not by activities such as yoga, but by pointless relaxing.

The light aroma of sulfur provoked in me Villon's verses. I don't consciously memorize anything. But I do have a habit of remembering—in this case, his "The Epitaph of Villon in the Form of a Ballade." Naturally, I recalled it in French, never having read it in translation. It seemed a maudlin theme for such a cheery day, as I glowed with euphoria—or "endorphins," as the Americans like to say. Yet I could not evade its stark, plain verses.

> *Vous nous voyez ci attachés cinq, six :*
> *Quant de la chair, que trop avons nourrie,*
> *Elle est piéça dévorée et pourrie,*
> *Et nous, les os, devenons cendre et poudre.*

Roughly:

> Look on us, five or six bodies strung up,
> A flesh from flesh each separately supped
> Now eaten piece by piece, to shred and rot
> As we give deadly bones to ash and dust.

It's what I wanted—not literal death, but to get leeched out, like the granite, to anticipate that inevitable passage, in a way that was more than an intellectual concept. More physical, less "neurological."

> *La pluie nous a débués et lavés,*
> *Et le soleil desséchés et noircis ;*
> *Pies, corbeaux, nous ont les yeux cavés*
> *Et arraché la barbe et les sourcils.*
> *Jamais nul temps nous ne sommes assis.*

The rain has washed and nitpicked us, the sun
Straight dried and blackened each one's skin,
Ravens and pies with beaks leave eyes skull-dug
Ripping beard and eyebrows, leaving crust.
Stood up, and never again to sit.

I smiled at the thought of clambering from the pool, a happy skeleton, dissolving to calcified white powder before the astonished eyes of other vacationers, all scrambling to the other end, as the distant whoosh of skiers picking a line down the mountain filled the sudden astonished silence. I am less enamored of the poem's pat ending, in which the criminals to be hung at the gallows cry out to Prince Jesus for forgiveness. As a "real" moment, of course I'm with them, but this poem is a brilliant construct which, like the sudden deathbed confession of a blackguard, leads to a trite, stock conclusion, bringing its ruder spirit down to the trivial level of many of Villon's contemporaries. He is, after all, the man who pungently and perfectly begins one ballad with "The goat scratches; it can't sleep." Add to that goat fleas, a cloven hoof, a habit of eating garbage, and you've got not Christ Our Lord, but the Ballad of the Devil's Fart. It's said that he wrote the gallows poem while in jail awaiting the carrying out of his death sentence. But in a happy ending, the sentence was commuted, and he skipped town at the promising age of thirty-four.

❧

I have not, so far, found the spiritual inheritor of Villon in the United States. There are rogues, to be sure. There is a type that writes directly out of personality, staging a continuous show of hard living captured on a bar napkin. The god of these, it seems, is Charles Bukowski, whose primary credentials were bad skin, being rejected by women, dropping out of Los Angeles City College, becoming an alcoholic, getting his work rejected continuously, and publishing in "underground" presses—what in France we would just call, "a literary publisher." I have met his followers, usually at university bars, and most of them are either studying in graduate programs in creative writing at research universities, on "miserable fellowships" (their words). Preferably, the bar serves bad beer (Tecate and Shiner are popular) at low prices, and there is a worn pool table in sporadic use. The tabletops should be sticky, and the floor swept infrequently. Chuck would have wanted it that way.

At one such bar, I invited myself to a table of these students, and bought everyone a round of the good stuff (nobody refused). After another couple of rounds, and me answering the usual questions about my provenance and itinerant resume (that brought me some cred), I noted that one of them was holding a book of Bukowski's poems. I asked him to read one aloud, and he brightened up. In fact, all of them did. He went straight to what he claimed was his favorite poem by any poet, living or dead. And he began to intone it, his voice becoming gravelly, as if he were channeling Good Time Charlie.

> don't ever get the idea I am a poet; you can see me
> at the racetrack any day half drunk
> betting quarters, sidewheelers and straight throughs,
> but let me tell you, there are some women there
> who go where the money goes, and sometimes when you
> look at these whores these onehundreddollar whores
> you wonder sometimes if nature isn't playing a joke
> dealing out so much breast and ass along the way

I asked the group if they were poets. Five said yes, one no, two remained silent. I asked them what was so great about Bukowski, and after a brief moment looking offended at my inane question, the book owner answered "He lived life. And he wrote it down."

"And what is life?" I wondered aloud. "Being drunk half the day, playing the ponies, bedding whores?"

"That's part of it," answered one.

"And you've been with prostitutes?" Another raised his hand. "A hundred dollar one?"

"No, it was only forty."

"And the rest of you, why haven't you indulged? Isn't that a rite of passage? A sentimental education? Part of becoming a real poet?"

"Well, you don't really need to do that now."

"I see. Because the breast and ass gets dealt out on or near campus?"

"Well—yeah. It's grad school."

They wanted to know whether I was a poet as well. I said yes, and they asked, a published one? I assented. That got a glance of respect and they bought me a round. As we waited for the Shiners to arrive, Tod, the owner of the book, asked me whether I'd ever been with a prostitute. "Yes," I answered. "A few times."

"A hundred dollar one?" More robust laughter, the sparkling eyes of youth, even when they're high.

"We pay in francs, but it was a lot more than that." A long whistle. Now they were impressed. "However, I didn't make a poem of the experience. It was a commercial transaction." That statement killed the buzz. One of them, grasping at straws, asked whether he could buy one of my books— whether I had one with me. I said I had exactly one copy, which I would gladly offer as a gift, but it was in French. His enthusiasm visibly dimmed, but he accepted it out of politeness.

Before I took my leave, I asked whether any of them had ever heard of François Villon. They had not. "My compatriot," I said. "One of the most brilliant poets of all time. He drank to excess, frequented prostitutes, in fact somewhat lived among them. He stole money, was involved in many brawls and he killed a man. He was thrown into prison with a death sentence, at only 34 years of age. At the last minute, the King pardoned him. A man's man."

Several shook their heads in approval. "I bet he's a hell of a writer."

"He is. Now him you can get easily in translation. Don't forget—Villon."
Many a hearty farewell handshake followed. As I rose to put on my coat,
Tod rushed forward, gave me a quick embrace and handed me the tome of
Bukowski's verse. And the next day, I read the whole thing.

The Barista

Not long ago, I read a report, one of those meant to invoke alarm and despair, about the decline of the liberal arts in American universities. The former purpose of college, it said, was to write, understand history, and philosophize. Now, those dedicated to the humanities had fallen by 15%--or maybe it was 50%. Either way, the news was dire. One major cause, it lamented, was that those who pursued this path ended up as poetry-spouting baristas.

Having perused numerous essays on the "death of" the arts, humanities, and of books, even, I am reminded of the lyrical gem of my alter ego, José Alfredo Jiménez, *Estás que te vas y te vas y no te has ido.* His country honors him precisely because he was a do-nothing with a permanent hangover who ended up writing his country's unofficial anthem, "El Rey." If we don't want to take our cue from an inspired barfly, maybe we can listen to Nietzsche when he says "We artists! We moon-struck and God-struck ones! We death-silent, untiring wanderers on heights which we do not see as heights, but as our plains, our places of safety!"

Yesterday, sitting at my usual perch in the Urth Café, where I like to watch humanity go by, often well-dressed in curve-enhancing dresses or ego-enhancing suits and ties, I looked up toward the counter, from the diaries of Witold Gombrowicz I was reading, and my barista, Stephanie, was spouting poetry. Staring directly at me, she mouthed syllables I was able to read across the room above the insistent grind of the espresso machine. They were two verses of Jules LaForgue. *Rien ne les tient, rien ne les fâche / Elles veulent qu'on les trouve belles.* They only want to be beautiful, with their Bachelors in Russian and Colonial History. Let the 80% or whatever per cent it is be engineers and attorneys, accountants and physicians. Let them matter more, if they must. Some days, resistance is futile, and you must wait for a better day. They're going to run things no matter what, or else the rest of us must sacrifice all our gods on the altar of scientific pragmatism and commercial resourcefulness and enter a race which we are foreordained to lose.

Perhaps Stephanie wasn't thinking any of these gloomy thoughts. She was smiling, she even winked at me, her poetic accomplice, secure in her unadorned youth. There is no cloak as magic as being 23 years old, skin and soul unblemished. The many times over the past year I've given her the order for my small Americano, room for cream (superfluous since she knows my order in advance), she's never once asked me what I do. She only jokes that I'm neither small nor Americano. As soon as I spoke, the first time I ordered, she said, without hesitation, "You're French!" as if I hadn't known it. She announced it to the world with a carefree insouciance, as if I'd won a prize, making all of us in the line laugh. As a result, when I appear each day, various and sundry wave and smile at me, "the Frenchman," calling me "Monsieur." Everyone is in on the game; everyone feels that suddenly we are on the Champs Élysées instead of Colorado Street. We welcome, tacitly, the fact that we too have a café society, just like those poets we're always hearing about, the ones who are trying to write in ateliers before climbing downstairs to smoke with their friends, or else they're writing in the halls of the foundering liberal arts colleges.

Stephanie recites poetry for the customers, not in the least embarrassed. It could be Roethke or Vallejo. It could be Dickinson or Petrarch. It could be Verlaine or Laforgue. She does it from memory. The regulars are used to the high-spirited, "crazy" barista, assuming that she simply must be in love, and wondering what verses she will drop on them today. She never asks me "what I do." That social tic I find eminently and rudely American. At every cocktail hour, dinner party, or barbecue, it is the first question. We must account for ourselves. We are identified by our work—better said, our pay stub, and there is no getting around it. It is not enough to understand history and to philosophize while you brew specialty drinks.

What would they say if they knew that many days, I walk around observing passersby, and sometimes write about them, extrapolating a life from a pair of shoes and an overcoat? I believe they'd find this activity suspiciously unacceptable, as if I were a spy. Which in fact I am. I've taken to telling people I'm a language tutor for school children in Brentwood and Bel Air. That draws a satisfied nod. If I am not rich, at least I am drawing off the stream of the rich, as their supplicant by teaching children a language for which they have no aptitude and will never use. It is assumed I will soon be teaching at a private school such as Harvard-Westlake, the practitioner of a devalued profession in a prestigious institution. This in turn allows me to be despised and patronized with the greatest cordiality. Their offhand contempt could not be more cheerful. I don't take it personally. They are really thinking about which investment will make their taxes lower, so they barely perceive me, now that I have answered their first question, the only one that matters.

I turn back to my tome of Gombrowicz, that ungrateful immigrant, that irascible prophet wearing bad clothes, a host of numerous physical tics, that biter of the hand that fed him—that small god who never let anyone around him grow comfortable. He had a maddening way with the truth:

What sort of attack can this kind of art dream of if it cannot defend itself and is already half-conquered?

I expect that in years to come art will have to shake off science and turn against it—this clash will take place sooner or later. Then there will be an open battle, with each side completely aware of its cause.

Gombrowicz and the Barista—they are more alike than different. It's true, he is a bad cold and she is the homeopathic remedy. He is a foreigner and she's at home alongside the hiss of the foam. He is a gadfly and she a butterfly. Yet both are poets out of joint with time, singing a prophecy that won't be listened to, or at best, overheard among the immediate din of those who await the small consolation of a warm cup in the hand, and don't necessarily want to look further.

Perhaps the day will arrive when Stephanie no longer quotes Laforgue, or even Jacques Prévert, because she has taken two additional part-time jobs to pay off her student loans and make rent on a shared apartment, and there is no energy, no voice leftover from asking us whether we want her to leave cream for our coffee. Or will she rise up, not as workers do against tyranny, but as geese do from a silver lake, their secret purpose spoken to each other in a language we must strive to understand?

The Soap Slides

Someone overnight sticks a gigantic
piece of carbon paper on my door.
Everything I am thinking immediately
comes through the other side of the wall.

Inquisitive people from all over the place
come in throngs. I hear the soles of their shoes
lift up the stairs to my apartment
and, leaving,
put them down again.

They are birds of every species,
moon farm dogs,
transitions, forest aisles and
old acacias that suffer from insomnia.

They put on spectacles and
read me, are moved or
threaten me with their fists, it
depends for I have a
clear idea of it all.

Only about my soul
I know nothing. About my soul that perpetually
slides away from me between days,

like a cake of soap
in the bath.

These are the words of Marin Corescu, his poem "Carbon Paper." Though the verses ought to feel foreign, descriptive of Romania under Nicoalae Causescu, in fact the scenario seems quite familiar, reminiscent of America at the present time. Except the carbon paper has taken on subtle forms; it leaves no smear. Today, predictive verbal software and the incursions of the NSA into our telephones and laptops bleed the brain. Amid the surveillance and the faceless anticipation of each word we are about to type, there sits a curious lack of danger about what is thought and said by almost everyone. Not knowing how to speak is expedient, even cheerful. Each virtual conversation, each post, has a numbing verbal similarity to the previous one. The impoverishment of language appears greater than ever before, because its users seem mentally exhausted. It's hard to be subversive—really subversive—at the present time, because in part, it's hard to find a discourse free of trivial insights framed in trite language. You can only yell a credo, or yell back a counter-credo, as if you were shouting on the shore of a lake at an imagined interlocutor, and the echo across the water endlessly returned and departed, until you could no longer make out the words.

I have been keeping a long list of the terms that represent the most banal thoughts I hear around me, ones so empty of content they are a slosh of backwash in a gallon plastic jug left in the sun, beginning to leech out its toxins. I won't bore you with them here—too numerous to mention. This dissolution of eloquence cannot all be blamed on the predictive software that knows what we are about to type and uses an algorithm to do it for us or narrows it down to two or three options. If anything, we are being reminded that we keep saying the same thing, cell phone or no cell phone.

Into this dilemma, from the past, steps Corescu, coming at us sidewise. His terrain is the absurd, moon farm dogs and insomniac acacias—as far from an earnest manifesto as one can get. Just when his poem seems to be a mere parable of resistance, the speaker turns it on himself, musing that

"Only about my soul/I know nothing." The authorities are never mentioned directly, only "someone." And I appreciate the deliberate vagueness, leaving open the possible conclusion that the issue is as much "us" as "them." More intriguingly still, he compares his soul sliding away to "a cake of soap in the bath." His essence will float on water, as souls might well do, yet it is material; it will dissolve.

As such, I began to wonder whether earnest American poetry has reached an impasse between the urge for linguistic self-renewal and casting off obvious meaning, on the one hand, and plain poetry that insists on its right to simply, and often without a single memorable image, declare an unjust state of affairs without caring about its assertions' capacity to surprise. I will admit that, having tried many times, I can never get far with Luis J. Rodríguez.

> Here is the Watts of my youth,
> where teachers threw me
> from classroom to classroom,
> not knowing where I could fit in.

The sentiment is valid, but if the line breaks are removed, it is nothing but a sentence—one of legitimate complaint, lacking the spark that might separate it from a civic speech, or the news, or that could not have been produced by the right kind of matrix, one programmed to recombine phrases of the socially aggrieved.

Langston Hughes, he of "I, Too, Am America," sometimes spoke in indignant platitudes, and sometimes spoke what needed to be said and hadn't been said. I find him most satisfying when he remains of easy apprehension, yet suggestive, respectful that poetry is comprised of tact regarding language.

> Must be the black Maria
> That I see,
> The black Maria that I see—
> But I hope it
> Ain't comin' for me.

There it is, philosophy or the worried blues—what's the difference? And mystery is preserved. He could be a social outcast, or prey to a disease, or simply paranoid. We may take our pick. We're not subjected to a set of stated facts.

Unless poetry can carry us over these chasms of thought masquerading as noble sentiment, devoid of verbal self-awareness, we might as well throw it over, and remain reading self-satisfied blogs and other cybernetic forums that speak without irony of "adulting" and "curating" and other mind-numbing pseudo-concepts. Until then, I will stick with Corescu, and read his poetry with fresh eyes, as if he had just handed it to me across the dinner table.

Après Nous le Déluge

L ouis XV's lover, Madame de Pompadour, said these words best and most romantically. And who could blame her for such daring, after all she did for architecture, the decorative arts, and Voltaire? She dressed in pink to go with her pink phaeton and to catch the King's eye; he brought her venison and dressed as a yew tree. But that pregnant phrase—after us, the deluge— has another, biting meaning for Marx; a sorrowful, lonely one for D.H. Lawrence. And yet another for groups of poets I've known.

I will admit I am old-fashioned in the sense that I like my avant-garde art served with a side of continuity. And I have found America—poetic America—a place of dogmatism, in which one must pledge allegiance to a style, a group style even, amounting to an ideology. The so-called "language poets," or to type it as they prefer, in sheer semiotics, "L=A=N=G=U=A=G=E, were said to have (newly) disrupted the lyric "I". And I say, Good for them! That "I" needs to be poked, to be made to blink, every so often. Let it shed tears, the more so as it specializes in mourning and loss, elegy and sometimes lazy reverie. But are persons who continue to write as Roethke did, as Elizabeth Bishop, be shouted down as naïve tourists taking postcards of volcanoes off the rack?

Pound showed us the value of rupture, with his Vorticism, with Futurism. I would have found him unspeakably tedious. Yet I read most of the *Cantos*. Was there a man more deeply indebted to the classics than him? He made me wish I'd paid more attention in Greek and Latin classes as a a boy. The man cannot disrupt in fewer than three or four ancient languages.

We French have been as bad as anyone about these coteries that somehow become "schools." The Symbolists and Surrealists are only two examples of the desire to be together yet separate. There is a clear line of succession from Baudelaire to Mallarmé to Breton. They might as well have had the same bloodstock.

Mallarmé's surprising lodestone "Un coup de des" is prefaced with modesty, when he declares that "the ensuing words, laid out as they are, lead on to the last, with no novelty except the spacing of the text." He has no desire to overstate the case. He derives from Baudelaire, and in his turn, will usher in, perhaps unwittingly, Breton. Our habit of overthrowing our predecessors is more in the way of a strong disagreement at a family reunion. That "throw of the dice," the herald of modernism," has not, for me, as a gesture, yet been surpassed. It fractured time, but then it healed time.

> *Un coup de des jamais n'abolira le hazard*
> A throw of the dice will never abolish chance

May we remember those choice sonnets of his? The ones certain parties would deride as fin de siécle? As if by one century merely ending, innovation will appear in the next. The end of the century is as likely the herald of apocalypse. And everyone these days, it seems, wants to be the first to wade into the flood. One of my favorites of Mallarmé's sonnets begins thus:

> Victoriously the grand suicide fled
> Foaming blood, brand of glory, gold, tempest!
> O laughter if only to royally invest
> My absent tomb purple, down there, is spread.

I want to be interred in this purple tomb, be its color ever so gaudy. It is so caught up in beautiful excess it has no time for the quarrels of others, their backward-looking, bleary-eyed derision of its quaintness.

Breton, that genius of impudence, one can easily imagine him looking backward at Mallarmé, clear-eyed, smiling, addressing him directly:

    In the inviolate darkness
    I anticipate once more the fascinating rift occurring
    The one and only rift
    In the facade and in my heart
    The closer I come to you
    In reality
    The more the key sings at the door of the unknown room
    Where you appear alone before me.

That is honor. That is realism. He looks askance only to draw nearer to his putative foe. That is—dare I say it?—manners. Even as we disrupt, explode, throw our fists and swear, we must recognize that this need to slay those around us, and before us, as something of a tantrum among educated people pretending to be precocious brats. I say to the Hejinians, the Bernsteins, the Antins, the Armantrouts, and their legions of successors—for yes, there are now many thousands at the helms and in the pages of magazines and presses—it was all done before you came along. You added flour to the roux, no doubt, but you staged no revolution by putting equal signs between a kindergartner's alphabet blocks.

To say *Après nous, le déluge,* is to overreach. In these days of "branding" I personally prefer not to have a brand. Perhaps I am only derivative, but in each of my books, I change style, like a man who lives in one rental house after another. The process for me is one of constant self-reinvention, devoid of one-upmanship. I don't want to stay in one place; less run the risk of getting grouped with someone else, other than those predecessors I acknowledge, and those fellow poet-travelers whose preferences and tastes are unlike mine, so there is no chance of us claiming an ideology together. I consider this stubbornly non-committal streak a virtue. None of us is, or ever can be, the apotheosis of our art, and less so by banding together like cave dwellers cursing a lightning storm. I love no one so much as a contrarian. Even more, the one who will reject my devotion to his or her contrarian streak.

Kestrel Elegy

THE STREETS ARE MOSTLY EMPTY. I don't mind. I am a walker, and I find the city peaceable. I should have stayed at home writing drastic, prophetic words, to rival Camus's *The Plague*, speaking of watching "a feeling normally as individual as the ache of separation from those one loves, suddenly become a feeling in which all shared alike and — together with fear — the greatest affliction of the long period of exile that lay ahead."

But I'm no Camus. First, I stopped reading newspaper articles, then their headlines. I don't want to keep up with the body count or the infection rate. I know how bad it is, even before all the zeroes get added. I refuse to speak the first half of the virus's name, because I don't want to glorify it. I always washed my hands a lot, so that's nothing new. And six feet apart— that is the distance I like anyway, what I call the contemplative gap. I'm not the person you're likely to find in a nightclub. Conviviality writ small, I seek it, as the time when three newfound friends and I spent all night on a balcony in San Miguel de Allende, watching New Year's Eve fireworks go off in the distance, drinking tequila out of a handmade Talavera bottle, listening to *salsa brava*, then driving around at six in the morning, still a little tight, searching for breakfast. We finally got fed cold *huevos divorciados* in a cavernous restaurant with most of the lights off, only because the owner took pity on us, as if we were urchins.

I like watching people from across the street as they queue up for a block-buster movie involving superheroes mildly surprised to find themselves in the same picture, the kind I probably wouldn't enjoy, or a popular new restaurant in Koreatown. There is something endearing about everyone's quiet expectancy, their sense of belonging at a remarkable happening. It doesn't matter if the movie disappoints. They won't notice. They only want to be somewhere at the right time, even if it's not the rapture. I have been riding trains to this and that favorite neighborhood. I walked around Koreatown, until I arrived at a restaurant where I sometimes went for takeout, a place where patrons-in-waiting stood outside as long as two hours hoping to enter, staring enviously at the favored ones in the backlit picture window, already eating deceptively simple dishes, as those outside waited for their phones to buzz with an alert. Today, no one sits. A single overhead light left on illuminates a patch of the dining room. Everything looks remarkably clean and safe within. The eerily white tablecloths have the hue of moonlight falling on a bleached skull. Suddenly, for the first time, I wish to belong. But everybody else is at home, terrified or quietly resigned.

Only a year ago, *The Washington Examiner* ran an article, titled "Notre Dame—an Ineffable Sadness."

> The destruction of Notre Dame Cathedral is a shattering disaster almost impossible to put into words. For the crowds who gazed at the conflagration from the banks of the Seine, as for millions around the world riveted to their television screens, the sight was one of horror, bottomless sadness, abject helplessness.

That used to count as a catastrophe.

I had a habit of sitting outside that cathedral, on the steps, sporadically feeding birds and teaching myself to play the harmonica. I never got good at it, but the pigeons didn't seem to mind. A few times I went into Mass and listened to the congregation sing the Te Deum out of the Ambrosian hymnal. Those same rapt faces, the ones from the Korean restaurant, the nightclub, the cinema, singing together and reciting together, so sure of themselves. Then they, and everybody else, had to watch that magnificent edifice be gutted by wicked fire, destroying with it the same false sense of permanence that let them believe in a benevolent God in the first place. I was raised Catholic, so I should know better than to say these things. I should simply pray the way I was taught, before the skeptical seed sprouted in me.

> *Ô saint Antoine, le plus gentil des saints, ton amour de Dieu et de ses créatures t'a valu, sur cette terre, des pouvoirs miraculeux. Je t'implore d'intercéder en ma faveur.*

That's what we're all saying to ourselves, right? *Please intercede on my behalf.* I don't ask to go straight to the front of the line. I only want to get there before the eggs, toilet paper, and medical attention are gone. I only need a dozen eggs, two rolls, and one life.

I've been hiking in the Santa Monica Mountains, against the rules. There's nobody there. The wildflowers are bursting with color, canary yellow, fuchsia, blood red. There has been plenty of rain in recent weeks. The air has not smelled this fresh since I moved to Los Angeles. The drought and the wildfires from last season that pitilessly destroyed so many lives, so many millions of acres of forest and scrub, the ones referred to daily as apocalyptic, are barely a memory now, except to those who suffered their wrath directly, and those who responded. That particular plague was undemocratic. Yes, billionaires and the poor both got scorched. But not all of them. This virus seems to have more democratic intentions, sociology and statistics notwithstanding. Any of us could be fucked. Probably those fires will return, tenfold or twentyfold, and then it will really seem like the end of the world. In the meantime, we take hope in traitorous numbers.

As Camus often said, in so many words, it's a weird time. When someone walking a dog waves from me across the street, they seem to be sending out a subtle rescue signal. When the cashier shyly greets me behind her mask at the grocery, she appears on the verge of speaking an elegy.

I have no taste for elegies. I'm certainly not writing one here. I possess a sensibility that is half optimism and half fatalism. That odd combination keeps me in good spirits. I don't expect the worst to happen. But when it does, I'll be mentally prepared. I found my next-door neighbor the other morning digging weeds out of his yard with bare fingers, for quite some time. Finally, he turned and asked, "What are you looking at?" I wasn't sure. I thought perhaps he had buried Federal treasury bills in a jar, or that he was trying to get to the center of the earth. I asked if I could help him. He said that was okay, as long as we remained as far apart from each other as the wingspan of three American kestrels, flying abreast. He didn't say where they were going.

Park for a Sleeping Man

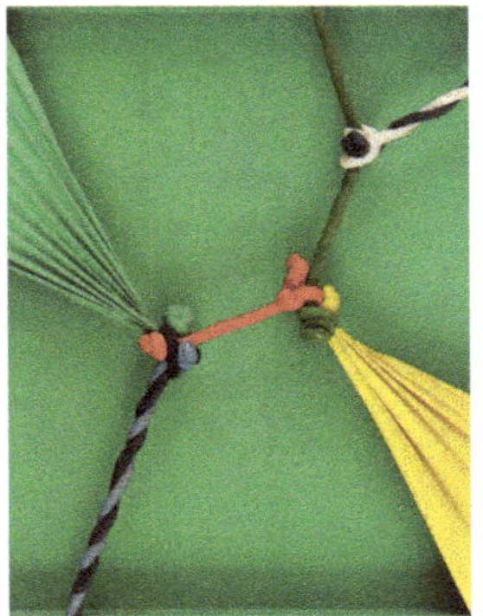

T HIS CREATION'S LEGEND: "Recently astrophysicists tell us that the universe is an infinite number of knots, created and dismantled without a break, and it's not possible to see the beginning or the end. In Stephan Georges' words, 'big thoughts arrive with dove's feet.'"

I was living back in Paris, having wrangled another newcomer grant—at my age—and took a short trip to Italy. I could feel a cold coming on, and with the wish-magic of a child, I tried to shake off infirmity by getting on a train where the wind whistled up and down the corridors, flowing from secret apertures. Once arrived, I spent an hour contemplating a modern variation on the ancient signifying Incan knot, the khipu. The objet d'art above, hung in a gallery in Firenze, was wrought by the Peruvian poet and artist Jorge Eduardo Eielson.

Returning to Paris, to the lodgings of a deceased aunt whose property was still tied up in probate, its French provincial furniture straight out of *Madame Bovary*, begging to be auctioned, I contemplated myself in the dresser mirror, the kind with a sheen that makes you look five years younger and like you don't have a cold. A single short sentence from that novel stabbed at my brain like an ice cream headache. "She wanted to die, but she also wanted to live in Paris." I knew exactly how she felt. I had returned to see whether the city fit me, or I it. It did not, and I did not. Why did I continue my peripatetic ways, in and out of beautiful but doomed relationships, like an adolescent? I was no less romantic or gullible than Bovary, that clueless matron who epitomized bourgeois conformism and deluded sentimental clichés.

The dying part—I'm too emotionally lazy for that. It could only happen if I were a ring of gas on a stove that someone absently flipped off while trundling back to the television with his tea. In that sense, I'm perfectly safe and not tormented, only prone to senseless melancholy floating up from the bottom of the koi pond that is me, a half-detached lotus flower, you can see the sheen of incipient rot, yet it's alive, forced to be so, and the rest of the pond exerts its silent might, the goldfish, the leaves, the gently burbling water spreading its mineral sediment, the dragonfly a little hexagram of inspiration, the wind freshening the sun-splashed surface. Ultimately, I am forced to be moderately happy, like Madame B on her best days. I am the least fit for the destiny of a tragic heroine. The universe, that endless knot of khipus, silently and secretly binds me together again.

That night, I slept poorly, enduring swirling visitations of great import, remembering none of them within two minutes of waking up. I craved a breakfast of crusty bread and coffee. I skipped it and instead, I went straight to a nearby bookstore where I'd always wanted to tread and asked for a volume, any volume, of verse written by Eielson. Marguerite, the owner, introduced herself and smiled as if she'd been waiting years for someone to make that request. Her eyes flickered and she reached underneath the counter, as one might have done in time past to pull out an antique magazine of soft pornography for sailors, or a small packet of marijuana, or "the good stuff," whatever that might mean. In this case, it was Eielson's 1954 *Via della Croce*, first edition, immaculate condition, signed by the author, the signature made of elegant knots like those of his khipu art.

Without asking the price, I handed her my debit card. "Cash only," she said, radiant, like one speaking to a fortunate disciple.

"How much?"

"How much do you have on you?" We blinked at one another, me not quite believing the conversation that was happening.

"You're really asking me that."

"I'm really asking."

"I happen to have withdrawn a lot of money from the bank, because not visiting France except fitfully, I am forever under the illusion that this nation is living under the Vichy government, long before I was born, and that a German junior minister will walk up to me on the street and demand I pay tribute in gold coins or the equivalent."

"How much tribute is that?"

"About five thousand francs."

"The book is worth that much. Maybe not on the rare book market, but to me it is."

"I can't afford that price, but I'll pay it if I must, because your arbitrary and unreasonable attachment to this particular volume of poetry—not a single word of which I've read, and which I can probably find free, digitized on the internet—moves me."

"Is that a yes?"

"I'll pay it." I opened my wallet and began to count my francs.

"What's your name?"

"Étienne d'Abattoir."

Marguerite touched my hand. "I have a single copy also of your book *Suivre.*"

"That's a miracle. There weren't that many printed, unless you have it in that bad German translation, full of errors and false cognates."

"In French, of course. But it's not signed. I'm going to give you this copy of Eielson. It needs to be read. Don't protest otherwise. In return, you will sign this copy of *Suivre.*"

"Thank you for your generosity. I didn't know my signature is worth that much."

"Only to me. Again, the vagaries of the market." I signed. My signature, bunched up in some places and overly loose in others, was no match for Eielson's, with his hand of a visual artist. "Now, have a seat in that comfortable chair and read a few of his poems, while I tend the counter and surreptitiously watch small expressions of pleasure and other emotions cross your handsome and sensitive face."

I had never been courted in this precise way. It seemed a more intimate connection between us had been decreed by the voluble yet immediate laws of the poetic sphere. At first, I kept an eye out, watching her watching me, trying not to preen when I turned the pages. I soon forgot her and got lost on the path of Via della Croce.

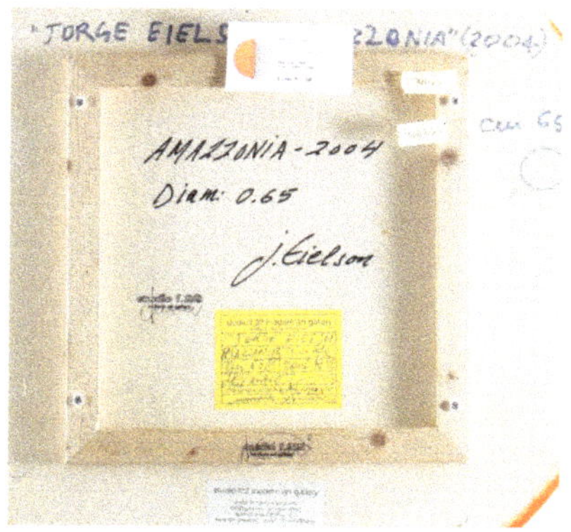

Park for a Sleeping Man

frecuentemente
cuando estoy sentado
en una silla
y estoy solo
y no he dormido
ni comido ni bebido
ni amado
tengo la impresión
de caer en un abismo
amarrado a mis vestidos
y a mi silla
y de irme muriendo suavemente
acariciando mis vestidos
y mi silla
tengo la impresión
de caer en un abismo
y de improviso asistir
a una remota fiesta
en el fondo de una estrella
y de bailar en ella
tiernamente
con mi silla

often
when I'm slouched
in a chair
and all alone
and haven't slept
nor eaten nor slaked
nor am loved
I have the sense
of falling into an abyss

tied to my shirt
and my chair
and that I'm dying slipping
caressing my clothes
I have the sense
of falling into an abyss
and on the sudden
heading to a fiesta
at the bottom of a star
and dancing inside it
tenderly
still in my seat

If I'd been a critic, I might have found fault with this verse, its simplicity possibly studied or on the contrary, unfiltered and unedited. I had in that moment the translator's bad habit, like a misbehaving child, to "improve" the text. Having moved like a hummingbird through many formalisms, threads of experiment, and the often-facile pranks of the Dadaists and Surrealists, never able to touch down for long on any single one, I ought to have been skeptical of this artless poetry that might well be mocking me. Unfortunately, it *was* me. And to critique it, I'd first have to look deep into myself to understand why I was willing to overvalue the poem far beyond its market price. My three best books didn't net me five thousand francs all taken together.

I let myself slip into the poem's uncanny foreknowledge that I'd be sitting in this very chair, dancing at the bottom of a star, albeit Marguerite had in fact directed me here and slid my index finger into those exact two facing pages, as if guiding me gently into her sex, so in truth she was fabricating the experience, manipulating me into this sensory identification. But it was far too real to shrug off as a trick. Her gaze, sly and hooded, was that of a fertile magician. Those *khipus*, with their sinuous knots, beyond her ministrations, were determining the course of events. I stopped my train of thought before I concluded that I was in fact Eielson.

After I stood up and put the book into my faded leather satchel, the one that had gotten scuffed in so many overhead bins, she locked the front door and whispered "*Suivre*," and I did just that. I followed her into her upstairs apartments—of course they would be there, an extension of the bookstore. We made love together, as if seeking physical connection between two old friends who could manage the passion leading to a burst of ecstasy in such a way that it wouldn't lead afterward to tears or confession. I loved on her imperfect body, and she on mine.

In that way I ended up in Cusco, sitting on a rooftop facing Salkantay Peak, the formidable snow abode of the mountain god. Marguerite had expected my departure from France, even silently encouraged it. That improvised voyage went with her Casablanca idea that "we'll always have Paris," in this case literally. I lodged at a hostel the first few nights, in part to see what that was like, in part to receive the bewildered but not unkind glances of the twenty year old backpackers, fresh off the Inca Trail, browsing Trip Advisor on their cell phones, at the sight of me, far better dressed than the occasion called for, my shirt pressed and my sleek black jacket spotless. These younger men wandered around the inner courtyard, often shirtless, showing off in the casual manner of prowess that takes itself for granted, while overhead squawked restless parrots in cages.

The price of a stay in the hostel was absurdly low and included an inedible meal of chopped, greasy beef on an unmade bed of stir-fried vegetables, which I handed to whomever sat across from me at the long, hard-seated aluminum table. We were in a commune of sorts, one in which the inhabitants changed every day or week. They spoke of trips to take ayahuasca with a licensed shaman. I didn't know that magic medicine men needed to be licensed. Everyone down to a person seemed happy in the recounting of their hallucinogenic experiences, which sounded more homeopathic than psychedelic. Nor were they, judging from expressions of placid oblivion and discussions about the next neo-European or neo-indigenous dance bar on the list to knock out, likely to identify with Walter Benjamin's assertion that "under hashish we are rapture-prosed beings of the highest power." They sought dark crowded places where the inability to hear each other over the blast of the music created an instant emotional Esperanto, destined to end in libidinal seizure.

It is for this reason, rather than because of physical discomfort and excessive accidental physical contact in the hostel, that I repaired to accommodations more suitable to my status as a bourgeois gypsy. I was eager to rid myself of the sound of buzzsaws from a new two-star hotel going up on one side of the hostel, and the jackhammers of street repair on the other. I moved to the outskirts of town, San Sebastian, into a tasteful Spanish style hotel with a quiet interior courtyard and a firm mattress on which I could sprawl while returning to the words of Eielson. I'd searched for bookstores in the warren of streets around the plaza, down Avenida Sol, and up the cobblestone jirones climbing toward Barrio San Blas, with its gastro-cafes and plethora of gift shops and endless window displays of machine-made alpaca shawls. I found nothing worth reading. I entered an interior courtyard selling stuffed rocoto, dodging two of the innumerable "comfort women," most of whom strolled the main square and adjacent, holding up laminated placards and repeating, in mechanically "alluring" voices, "Massage, massage…Massage, massage." I assumed that a spectrum of services was available, but my decided evasion of eye contact left that matter a blessed mystery for the health inspector.

In a stall in the back lay yet another redundant tourist agency, offering the same eight excursions as all the rest, at the same price. It was empty, save a lone representative, maybe the owner, gazing at nothing, not even me. He could have been channeling the collective spirit of his ancient Tawantinsuyo brethren; but I believe he was only bored. Behind him sat a makeshift bookshelf of crates, and into them had been deposited books old and new: novels of Danielle Steele and Tom Clancy, a paper Lonely Planet guide far out of date; a variety of ersatz tomes that had the word "Inca" in the title.

Squeezed among them was a handful of works of Peruvian literature, all quite old and with bindings about to give. One of them was called *Vuelta a la Otra Margen* (*Return to the Other Shore*). Its date was 1970, from Casa de la Cultura. Without reserve, I paid the ten dollars asked. The cover is an appealing black and white, the size to hold in one's hand like a breviary, with a woodcut-style inset of a man's silhouette, bowler hat, standing at the back of a Chinese junk with a canopy, on still reflective water. The effect is one of discreet, contemplative, *chinoiserie*. At the top, in block letters run together, were the last names of six poets, one of them Eïelson.

Back in my room, a fresh, high altitude breeze coming between the iron bars, me propped up on tapestry pillows, I opened the book, slowly so as not to crack the binding further. Already a few pages were loose, and I hoped that none had gone missing. On the first page was a poem by césar moro (lower case, as if to invite tact).

> *L'amour dédicace à l'amour*
> *Les jours sans pluie*
> *Et comme il convient les beaux jours*
> *Pour l'amour et ses préférances...*

I continued to read in amazement. This initial poem of the anthology was written in my native language. Unlike Vallejo, who had become more Peruvian the longer he languished in Paris, Moro had adopted French as a co-equal poetic language. I was reminded of the close correspondence between our two poetic cultures.

Soon I turned to Eielson (in Spanish), discovering possibly the most beautiful poem in the Spanish language. Many will disagree, yet it is satisfying to assert one's irrational, spontaneous sense of things, replacing any possible objective criteria with my supreme taste and the emotional vibrations of the moment. As such, that transcendent poem must be read whole, not cited.

Parque Para un Hombre Dormido

Cerebro de la noche, ojo dorado
De cascabel que tiemblas en el pino, escuchad:
Yo soy el que llora y escribe en el invierno.

Palomas y níveas gradas húndense en mi memoria,
Y ante mi cabeza de sangre pensando
Moradas de piedra abren sus plumas, estremecidas.
Aun caído, entre begonias de hielo, muevo
El hacha de la lluvia y blandos frutos
Y hojas desveladas hiélanse a mi golpe.
Amo mi cráneo como a un balcón
Doblado sobre un negro precipicio del Señor.

Labro los astros a mi lado ¡oh noche!
Y en la mesa de las tierras el poema
Que rueda entre los muertos y, encendido, los corona
Pues por todo va mi sombra tal la gloria
De hueso, cera y humus que me postra, majestuoso,
Sobre el bello césped, en los dioses abrasado.

Amo así este cráneo en su ceniza, como al mundo
En cuyos fríos parques la eternidad es el mismo
Hombre de mármol que vela en una estatua
O que se tiende, oscuro y sin amor, sobre la yerba.

Park for a Sleeping Man

Brain of the night, golden eye
Of chimes you tremble in the pine, listen:
I am the one who cries and writes in winter.

Doves and snowy steps sink into my memory,
And before my head of blood thinking
Stone dwellings open their shaken feathers.

Park for a Sleeping Man

Still fallen, among ice begonias, I move
The rain hatchet and soft fruit
And leaves unveiled turn frosted at my blow.
I love my skull like a balcony
Folded over a black precipice of the Lord.

I carve the stars by my side oh night!
And on the table of the lands the poem
Rolls among the dead and, lit, crowns them
So my shadow passes through all, such glory
Of bone, wax and humus that prostrates me, majestic,
On the beautiful grass, scorched by the gods.

Thus I love this skull in its ash, like the world
In whose cold parks eternity is the same
Marble man watching within a statue
Or who lies, dark and without love, on the grass.

Deliberately I tried not to understand this poem, availing myself of the powers of mind I have trained over the years to treat a poem as an experience, devaluing any semantic meaning. Nonetheless it described my current state exactly. Marguerite had known what she was doing when she lured me to her shop—how, I couldn't fathom—expressly to get me to Peru, into that tour guide's shop, wherein I would discover the second waiting book and be reading this poem at this exact moment, as gelid air blew harder through the windows, announcing nightfall. She was a shaman, but not the licensed, hygenic kind that the esoteric tourists were paying to see. I didn't need either hashish or ayahuasca to penetrate into my own core, to become that lotus flower that was half rotting and trying to re-attach itself fully to its pad, or else decay into vegetable matter. No, my metaphor was all wrong. It was what Eielson said, bone, wax, and humus that prostrates me, majestic, on the beautiful grass.

The rain hatchet blew up and hurled itself through the window, narrowly missing me, only its spray bathing my face. Or was that sweat ? Astrophysics, I know nothing about it. Isn't it enough to be able to write Alexandrine syllabic verses if you want ? Was more required of me than competing with this one by Baudelaire ?

> La très-chère était nue, | et, connaissant mon cœur
> Elle n'avait gardé | que ses bijoux sonores
> Dont le riche attirail | lui donnait l'air vainqueur
> Qu'ont dans leurs jours heureux | les esclaves des Maures.

> My most beloved was bare | she knew my heart's desire
> All she wore were jewels, | jingling gems of fire:
> Her naked garment lent| a conqueror's conceit,
> Or Moorish slave girls' joy | who snatch love from defeat.

Baudelaire, my tutelary spirit, hearkened to me with those verses. He was speaking of Giselle in Dubrovnik, though he could know nothing of her existence, nor of mine, unless out of time. There was no escaping her in dream or fantasy. I would displace him, and her, with a counter-poem of my invention.

> Canard torrent, nandou Darwin, haute tête blanche-noire,
> des plumes dans piscine, tourbillon en fin roché fendue
> deux ailes banales, ormes noirs soulèvent des bras tordus.
> Hache tranche, je fends pierre dure, mes membres nus rampent lents,
> Là où je m'accroupis, bois pastorale sanglante.

> Torrent duck, Darwin's rhea, its white-black head aloft,
> its feathers spill to pool, last whirl into cleft rock
> two wings banal under black elms lifting crooked arms.
> Ax sharp, I split stark stone; my naked limbs slow crawl,
> To where I crouch and drink in bloody pastoral.

A woman in the plaza unrolled a wall-hanging before me, made of multicolored yarn squares, seven across and seven down: yellow-orange-red-purple-green-white. A flag she said, called a wiphala, of the Quechua and Aymara. The woman, small, slender, eyes placid and playful, ones that had doubtless made for an easy marriage, explained that it came out of prolonged social struggle. She spoke with the poise and eloquence of someone who should have gone to college. What made me buy it was her telling of how her family created them, with pride and care. Its stitching wouldn't separate even in twenty years. The quality of dye ensured the colors would not fade. This "same" object I'd seen being sold by many was a different one. They considered themselves artists as well as artisans. She sold me their gourds as well, delicately steel-needle etched with a Japanese miniaturist precision, depicting scenes of Andean history and of her hometown, Ollantaytambo. Feli was her name. She sat on a bench and discoursed with calm passion, not ideology but lived experience translated into an idea. Feli was in no hurry to sell. Her manner was far above that of the quick-exchange vendors congregated at the perimeter of the square, some of whom had accosted me with their wares two or three times in half an hour, not recognizing my face from the time before. Feli made direct eye contact, knowing her creations as a puppeteer does her puppet.

As with the edition of Eielson, I didn't ask how much. I only said I would pay whatever they were worth. Without hesitation, she named her price and I offered the required colored bills, not bothering to translate the transaction into dollars or francs. Wrapping up the gourds inside the wiphala, she handed them over. Then she reached into a small woven bag and took out a CD in a case with a faded label. "A gift. These songs were compiled by Jaime Guardia, the great charango player. This performance was recorded at a night party. If you listen closely, you can hear the firewood popping."

Back at my room, I sipped coca leaf tea my hostess offered. I asked if she had a CD player and she found one stashed away beneath the reception desk.

Munaspa suyaykuway
Wamanqa laymanta, kutimunaykama,
Arikipa lawmanta, weltamunaykama.

Qilluy, qilluy duraznucha,
pukay, pukay manzanacha,
¿pipaqtas, maypaqtaq qilluyakuchkanki?
¿Pipaqtas, maypaqtaq pukayakuchkani?

Qilluyaspa, qilluyaspa,
pukayaspa, pukayakuy.
Warma wiqiywancha reqapayasayki
Unchuchuchaykiway, chukuchallayki prestaykumay,
chukuchaykimay chukuykukuspay
kunan tutalla puriyrukusaq,
kunan tutalla pasyarukusaq.

Chiriwarachay, warachallayki prestaykumay,
warachaykiway waraykukuspay...
esquina tiendapi tiyaq niñachay,
traguchallayki prestaykuway.

Please wait for me, wait
Until I'm back from Huamanga
Until I'm back from Arequipa.

Yellow peach, yellow peach,
Apple so red, so red,
Who turned you yellow, made you wander?
Who made you walk, who turned you red?
Shining, shining,
Twinkling, twinkling.

With my young girl's tears, I wet your face
Chuchu bird, lend me your crown
I'll put on your crown

Tonight, I'll ramble
Tonight, I'll roam.

Billow-leg cold, loan me your pants
I'll wrap myself in cold-leg pants
Little girl sitting on the corner curb
I'll sip honey from your glass.

The beautiful thing about crying is we don't ask permission to do so. That I did, turning up the music so the tinny speakers might drown out the sound for the next guest over. He did knock softly on the wall, but I realized it was not to shush me; rather, he was letting me know that everything would be all right.

The reason I was able to translate the Quechua lyrics into English is because the innkeeper, Dorotea first translated them into Spanish for me. We sat in the courtyard together. She already knew the lyrics and sang them to herself as she instantly transmuted the words into written form in Spanish. I admired how she moved among three languages with the same ease as any European aristocrat. My continent is unreasonably proud of its multilingualism, comparing itself favorably to the U.S. and forgetting about the rest of the world.

That night, Dorotea invited me down to the lobby, where she'd made a fire. She took out a guitar and said she'd teach me another traditional song, in Spanish. Another couple sat on a nearby couch, pretending they weren't going to listen. I don't know why, but she asked me if I was a poet.

"Yes."

"I thought so." She told me to close my eyes so that I could catch the cadence and the rhythm.

Little hummingbird, where do you fly?
Little hummingbird, where do you fly?
Coast, mountains, jungle, then to the sky.
Coast, mountains, jungle, then to the sky.

Her finger strumming was smooth, her finger picking nimble. When she was done, she tried to hand me the guitar and I waved it off. "You don't play? I assumed you would."

"No."

"Sing, then."

"I don't really sing."

"Ah, *really* is the important part of that sentence." She began to hum to encourage me. I fell in, tentatively at first, then with more confidence. The couple on the couch smiled and so did Dorotea. I was surprised at the warmth of my voice. Dorotea clapped her hands to keep the cadence and applauded when my performance was done. "Étienne, in Cusco everyone sings and dances, well or badly. It makes no difference. It's like writing poems, I guess. You begin with awkward strokes, then it gets better. You made the three of us here happy. In the city center, you've seen dancers in costumes of the *p'asña, ukuku* and *majeño* showing up from all over the countryside, converging for the Inti Raymi, the Festival of the Sun? It's what we do. The barber and the schoolteacher. The banker and the fruit seller from the market. The child and the grandfather. And we don't dance for you. We do it for ourselves, and we invite you in. This is a fierce culture that withstood centuries of humiliation and didn't cave. We aren't rich, but we are us."

The next afternoon I lay in a hammock in the garden, watching a dozen or so hummingbirds taking turns at the feeders, their wings beating a smooth whir, like a mustache trimmer in the hands of that barber she mentioned. I'd stayed up half the night as dancers practiced in the dark square, for the coming parade past the judges on the dais being set up by day with hammers and drills, between the McDonald's and the ancient cathedral hewn of once-Incan stone. At 2 a.m. or so, I had to go to bed, but the young troupes of dancers, some in costume, some in street clothes, whooped and joked and leapt as their director reminded them to stay in rhythm with one another.

Park for a Sleeping Man

The first thing I did upon my return to Paris was go straight from the airport to Marguerite's book shop. There she stood behind the counter, attending to this and that patron, helping another search a bookshelf, benignly ignoring me. I grabbed a book at random, Jules Michelet's *The Bird*, and sat in my usual chair. I opened at random and read:

The black hour passes, day reappears, and I see a small blue point in the heavens. Happy and serene region, which has rested in peace far above the hurricane! In that blue point, and at an elevation of ten thousand feet, royally floats a little bird with enormous pens. A gull? No; its wings are black. An eagle? No; the bird is too small. It is the little ocean-eagle, first and chief of the winged race, the daring navigator who never furls his sails, the lord of the tempest, the scorner of all peril—the man-of-war or frigate-bird.

I couldn't help but think of my counter-poem about the torrent duck and Darwin's rhea, two birds of which I was not conscious of ever having heard of before I wrote about them. Then there was the CD of the wiphala seller, leading me to ask Dorotea for a translation, whereupon she sang about the hummingbird, so did I, and then I lay in the hammock as actual hummingbirds clustered. Could all this be accidental? Was it set in conscious motion by the khipu? What was it the astrophysicists said—big thoughts arrive with dove's feet.

At last the shop emptied, save me, and I followed Marguerite to the counter, as if I had a bone to pick, though I had none. She stood waiting for me to say something. I discarded the idea of talking about my sudden trip to Peru with the money I'd saved by not buying Eielson's book for five thousand francs. I noticed *Suivre* on the countertop. "Did you read it?" I asked, with more heat than I intended.

"I'd already read it several times before I met you. But yes, I've been enjoying it again, one poem at a time."

"How does it hold up? I'm not Eielson, I'm sure."

"You may be overrating him. I didn't appraise his book based on the poetry. It was the edition that interested me. As for comparisons, sometimes you surpass him and sometimes he surpasses you. In particular, I am drawn to your poem "Malgré Moi.""

"Thank you. I detested it at first sight. I rewrote it many times. It's my personal favorite—malgré moi."

"You'll be interested to know that since your book has been sitting here on the counter, several customers have tried to buy it. One man came back several times and kept upping his offer and I kept telling him it's a signed edition, almost one of a kind, and not for sale."

"How much did he offer?"

"At the end, five thousand francs. You're worth as much as Eielson. I declined to sell. He stormed off and promised never to patronize my shop again."

"You should have sold it. I probably have a copy stashed away somewhere I could give you, if I can only find it."

"Yours is probably dog-eared and thumb-loosened. I'm betting you're that kind of reader, and sometimes you feel insecure and reread your own words, trying to find the genius."

"That genius was never there."

"He's there. But I'm not going to tell you on what page."

"Are we about to make love again?"

"It depends on how late I end up closing. I'd say there's a chance."

"You sent me to Peru, didn't you?"

"I have no idea what you're talking about."

"The chair. Hunger. The abyss, the star. Khipus. Darwin. Feli. Dorotea. Hummingbirds. This book by Michelet about birds. Any of it ring a bell? I believe they all have a secret connection."

"You're free associating. Maybe it's the beginning of a new poetry collection."

"It doesn't matter. I brought you back a gift." I unpacked the wiphala and unfurled it. "This represents—"

"Don't tell me anything about it, Étienne. It's only an object for visual contemplation, like Eielson's khipus. Better that nobody can decipher them." She rummaged in the drawer for tacks and hung it on the wall right behind the cash register. "That brightens the space. I'll find a more suitable way of hanging it tomorrow."

"After we make love?"

She came around the counter and hugged me. "Yes, after that."

from Eielson's "mutatis mutandis," 1967:
Escribo algo
algo todavía
algo más aún
añado palabras pájaros
hojas secas viento
borro palabras nuevamente
borro pájaros hojas secas viento
escribo algo todavía
palabras

I write something
something more
still more
I add bird words
dry leaves wind
Once again I erase words
I erase birds dry leaves wind
I write something more

words
from *Suivre*:

Sous les branches souples
lambent et argent
sumac comme
cendres qu'on ne pas mange.

Chaque ciel garde-manger
les nuages coller
herbe ci-dessous gravé
en acide doux

Ces soupirs passés
dur comme des punaises
craquelé comme de la boue
des larmes comme des briques

comme des mèches
qui poussent
vers un troupeau
d'oies agitées.

Le remords est un bâton
cassé deux fois
une fois comme un élancement
encore comme le chaos.

Le premier coup de conscience
secoue la poussière de l'arbre
de la vie exposant
le squelette sous l'écorce.

Là encore, c'est doux comme de la tire
qui colle à chaque index
sondant ses entrailles

Park for a Sleeping Man

comme le sexe d'une femme.

Je suis susceptible de mettre un sort
sur quiconque souffre
mes tics anonymes
ou me renvoie aux étoiles.

C'est toi, mon amour
mon erreur pathétique
celui dont le parfum
défie les cheminées

qui me réclame
de la terre
et suit mon ombre
comme s'il était fait chair.

Under the supple boughs
lambent and silver
sumac as
inedible ash.

Each sky its own larder
the clouds of paste
grass below etched
in sweet acid

Those past sighs
hard as tacks
cracked as mud
tears as bricks

as the forelock
of yesterday presses
toward a flock
of restless geese.

Remorse is a staff
broken twice—
once as a twinge
again as chaos.

The first thwack of conscience
shakes dust from the tree
of life, exposing
the skeleton beneath bark.

Then again, it's soft as taffy
that sticks to each index finger
probing its innards
like a woman's sex.

I'm liable to put a hex
on anyone who suffers
my anonymous tics
or refers me to the stars.

It's you, love
my pathetic fallacy
the one whose perfume
defies smokestacks

who reclaims me
from the earth
and follows my shadow
as if it were made flesh.

       ❦

The wind is driving sharp, stinging ice and snow into our faces as we lean
into them to proceed down the street. The storm smells of the iron particles
of all the dead poets. Someday they'll be forged into a huge bell that will
ring from the top of a cathedral, tolling a secret language that only a few
will listen to and understand. A metal semaphore, patient in its attempt to

become one with the air before its notes decay. Something like permanence. Our faces are sheeting with ice. There is no point in Marguerite opening her bookstore today. Hardly anyone is on the street. I believe she'd go on walking if I did. She's short but her haunches are powerful as those of a greyhound. She wouldn't strike anyone who saw her in shorts as bookish.

I steer us into a café and at once her glasses steam up. Now she's a librarian about to start feeling the wall for a latch to the secret passage, the one that will lead us down corridors that end at the bottom of a star. I order us two extra strong coffees—actually, they're all extra strong, you just have to say "coffee." We stand huddled together as there are no seats. The bitterness of the coffee is sweet. I scald the roof of my mouth, a little, but I don't care. If the human vapor of this improvised shelter packed with thirty people draws any closer, she and I will become two stamping horses snorting steam from our nostrils.

Marguerite has taken it into her head that I am an important enough writer that she must start a small publishing venture and reissue all my books as a series under a single imprint. I am flattered, of course. But I question the wisdom. It's pressure. First, because we're sleeping together, and even though I didn't suggest the idea, it feels like a vanity project. She insists not. She wants to know why I should go on writing books until these get read properly. That question is not easy to answer, as I have asked myself the same question many times. Why be a poet at all? It's a malady of sorts. Reverse bibliomania. Of course, I want to be famous—but not really. I just want the books to fly out of their hiding places and into the arms of unsuspecting readers, without her or me having to do anything. Second, I object that I will begin to find fault with all of the poems as I return to edit them. I'll grow skeptical of my own creations.

"It would do you good to have a hard look. They're not perfect, you know." I give her a hurt look; I can feel it on my face. "Except for *Suivre*, of course. Which is worth five thousand francs—at least."

I can see her fantasy: lines outside the bookstore, her needing to hire another person, and not being afraid to use the phrase *profit margin* in company. There is no sense me trying to dissuade her. She is not only stubborn, but also powerful. Tilting her head, Marguerite rubs her knit hat into the chest of my wool coat, and I prickle with delight. Yes, we are those two aforementioned horses and soon we will shiver together, spraying drops over the assembled, eliciting surprised cries. A table opens up. A couple beside us looks our way, doubtful. At the same time, we wave them toward the table, and they do a little dance around us, our bodies almost touching, with smiles that are part friendly, another part agony. They sit and balance is restored.

Marguerite is complaining in a low voice that it's all social media now, publicity included—look at everyone buried in their cell phones. That's not only rude, it's bad for business—and for their spiritual development. They should all be reading poetry right now! Yours! Someone hears her and looks up apologetically, putting his phone away. Guilt—the great marketing strategy. Physical contact—with the book, after the author touches, signing it, after the seller brings it reverently from the stack. That would be the new-old consciousness. The readers with the live voice of the writer in their ears. "Like you, Étienne. I don't mean only the poet. I mean you and Jorge. I fell for you both when you were holding that copy of *Via della Croce* in your hands, lost already, on your way to Peru to listen to hummingbirds sing."

Johnny Payne is a poet, novelist, playwright, essayist, and librettist. He has directed his plays *Touchstone*, *Cannibals*, and *Los Feliz*. Payne is Director of the MFA Program in Creative Writing at Mount Saint Mary's University, Los Angeles. He is a native of Kentucky.